IN ARGYLL

Also by Lisa Tuttle

Horrorscope: Virgo
The Snake Inside

First published in Great Britain 1996
by Mammoth, an imprint of Reed International Books Ltd
Michelin House, 81 Fulham Road, London SW3 6RB
and Auckland, Melbourne, Singapore and Toronto

Copyright © 1996 Lisa Tuttle

The right of Lisa Tuttle to be identified as author of this
work has been asserted by her in accordance with
the Copyright, Designs and Patents Act 1988

ISBN 0 7497 2734 9

A CIP catalogue record for this title
is available from the British Library

Printed in Great Britain
by Cox & Wyman Ltd, Reading, Berkshire

Panther
in Argyll

Lisa Tuttle

MAMMOTH

To Nancy Smith, who saw the panther

Contents

Prologue

There must be people who live their whole lives with the unhappy feeling of being in the wrong place. They feel different from everyone around them, but they don't know why. They sense something missing but never understand what it is. They never know their own story.

This is mine.

1

A Different Country

According to my mother, the first person I ever properly smiled at after I was born was not her but her closest friend at the time, Claire Tinker.

Claire was my favourite person, my godmother, and my only baby-sitter for the first two and a half years of my life. I wailed whenever she left, and as soon as I could crawl, I made valiant attempts to follow her.

There are lots of family stories about my bond with Claire Tinker, but to me they were only stories. I had no memories of this woman, who had moved away from our Birmingham suburb, far away to Scotland, before I turned three. I had never seen her since, although every year she sent me a present on my birthday, and book-tokens at Christmas and Easter. She had often invited us to visit, but, although my mother had gone as far as making plans a couple of times, we'd never actually managed to get there.

I kept hoping. I didn't know if I believed the things my mother said about the special relationship I'd had with Claire, and even if it had been true, I was no longer an innocent two-year-old, I was coming up to my thirteenth birthday, and, to tell you the truth, by the time I was twelve I didn't feel that close to anyone. None of my primary school friendships managed to last out the final year, and the secondary school I went to, from necessity not choice, was a rundown, overcrowded, factory-like place where I knew no one and no one wanted to know me. Sure, I loved my parents, but they were like the residents of another planet, with their own language, and somehow when I tried to translate my thoughts into their words I almost never managed to say what I really meant. I occasionally wondered if Claire would be any different from my parents, or from any of the other adults I knew.

And then, suddenly, I got the chance to find out.

My mother, who had been trying to get her career as a commercial artist off the ground, had been offered a wonderful job which would mean spending nearly a month in New York. She couldn't take me with her, and she was worried about leaving me at home since my dad's job as a sales rep involves a lot of travel with occasional overnight stays. She was fretting about how 'lonely' and 'bored' I would be, as if that situation would be anything new. I expected my summer would be much the same wherever my mother was: long empty days which I would fill as best I could by reading, daydreaming and riding my bike.

'You could go to your Gran in Norfolk,' she said uncertainly. 'Maybe just for a week or two?'

There would be the seaside, but to set against that there would be my Gran's endless fussing, and never a peaceful moment to myself in the poky bungalow

4

with its smells of lavender soap, medicine and moth-balls. However, if I could go away—

'What about Claire Tinker?' I asked. 'She's invited us often enough. Do you think she might have me to stay?'

She would. Her voice on the telephone was husky and warm, telling me how happy she was that I wanted to come, and how much fun we'd have together, in her house overlooking the sea on the west coast of Scotland.

On the plane to Glasgow I couldn't concentrate on the book I'd brought as I imagined meeting Claire, looking at her and feeling the bond my mother had spoken about. I imagined it as a peaceful feeling. The understanding between us would be so deep that we would hardly need to talk.

My mum had given me a photograph of Claire taken about ten years ago. It showed a slim, smiling woman with straight, shoulder-length fair hair. But I knew I wouldn't need it to identify her. When the plane landed, I walked along the corridor towards the main concourse of the airport, certain that I would know her as soon as our eyes met.

Someone snatched at my arm and pulled me around. 'Danielle? Are you Danni? I'm Claire Tinker.'

A very tall, thin woman with short, straw-coloured hair and a pinched-looking face peered down at me through enormous dark glasses. She was a total stranger.

She didn't even smile at me. She seemed nervous, abrupt, her mind on other things. 'Did you bring your cases as hand-baggage? Oh, God. Well, come on, let's go and find them.'

She smoked, in defiance of the *No Smoking* signs everywhere, as we waited by the luggage carousel for mine to come around. She fired questions at me about the flight, my mother, my health and then didn't listen to my answers.

It was a relief when my big blue suitcase came trundling along, followed immediately by the smaller grey bag. 'Those two.'

She hauled them off. 'Oof. Ever hear of travelling light?'

'Mum said I should bring lots of warm clothes.'

'Mmmm, well, we're not in the Arctic Circle. Come on, this way.'

Her car was in the nearest car park, which was decorated with warning signs prohibiting stays of longer than twenty minutes. 'Phew,' said Claire. 'Just made it! Oh, how I hate airports! And crowds. Hop in and we can get out of here. Sorry if I seemed unfriendly – places like this put me in a state and I can't do anything but worry until I get out.'

An apology: so she didn't hate me. But still there was no rapport. That 'special bond' between us must have been in my mother's imagination.

I felt cold and sad and empty. The summer stretched ahead of me like a prison sentence. I should have gone to my Gran's, I thought – at least she loved me. I had so been counting on Claire turning out to be my friend and mentor and filling the gap in my life. Now that I knew she wouldn't, I couldn't think why I was here.

At first I was too locked in with my disappointment to notice what was outside the car. When I did, I saw beautiful scenery. There was a loch. Water, reflecting the changing sky above, surrounded by forested hills, then mountains stretching away in the distance.

And it went on. On and on, hills and trees and water and sky. No people. No buildings. It was like nowhere I'd ever been. I kept expecting the pretty bits to come to an end, overtaken by the sort of cityscape I thought of as normal. But it didn't. I wasn't at home any more. This was a different country.

Something inside me loosened and opened up in response to the beautiful wilderness. I felt happy and excited.

'Do you want to stop?'

Claire's voice startled me; I'd practically forgotten about her.

'We can stop here if you like.'

We had just rounded a bend, and the glittering water disappeared from view. Ahead I saw a sign advertising a hotel, and a petrol station. There was a row of houses on the other side of the road. I felt a clutch of disappointment. Back to the real world.

'It's just that if we don't stop here there won't be anything until Inverary, and that's the better part of an hour away.'

'I don't want to stop,' I said.

'Good. I do like to get through the Rest before

stopping . . . I don't feel I'm back in my own territory until I'm through the Rest and Be Thankful.'

The Rest and Be Thankful turned out to be a place – but not a place with buildings. It was a pass through the mountains. As we travelled along the high road, I twisted and turned and craned my neck to gaze up the slopes that rose so steeply from the roadside, feeling my heart pound with a joyful excitement. Waterfalls tumbled and spurted down the hillsides. Some of the slopes were bare and craggy with jutting rock, others were furred with deep green pine forests. Far below I could see a rocky, meandering stream cutting through a grassy field. The little white blobs against the green were grazing sheep. Nothing else of human civilization to be seen except the road we were travelling, and the other cars.

There was a gentle bump and the crunching sound of gravel beneath the tyres as the car slowed, jarring me out of my dream. 'What's wrong?'

Claire took off her dark glasses and smiled at me. Her eyes were a sort of faded blue, with darker blue around the rims of the irises. Beneath her make-up I could see lots of tiny lines scored into the fine skin near her eyes. She looked older than my Mum.

'You feel it, don't you?' she said. 'You're just as moved by this as I was when I first saw it. Such a shock, after all that tamed and civilized country down south! So much beauty – I nearly went off the road, my first time, trying to see everything, before I had the sense to stop. That's what these roadside viewpoints are for, so you can look your fill.'

'May I get out?'

'Go ahead. I'll sit here and have a smoke.'

Out of the car, I inhaled the cool, pine-scented damp air. It was cooler here than it had been in Birmingham, almost cold. But I didn't want to go back for the jacket I'd left on the back seat. I walked to the edge of the gravelled area and saw a path leading down the grassy glen. I could hear the sound of rushing water, like wind in the trees, and I stared across at the wooded hillside, imagining myself hiking up through the trees. I was excited by the thought of being alone and free in the wilderness. It didn't matter about Claire. I would be fine on my own. I was glad I was here.

A car went by on the road behind and broke my dream.

'Here you are,' said Claire when I got in, handing me a newspaper. She spoke in an aggressive, jolly voice that put my back up. 'That's my work, that is. What d'you think?'

'This is your paper?'

'Editor, chief reporter, and general dogsbody – I'm a regular one-man band. Except for the advertising. Somebody else handles that. Well, look at it! I'd like to know what you think.'

It was called the *Argyll Advocate*. The whole of the front page, except for an ad for a car dealer, was taken up by one story, headlined PANTHER IN ARGYLL: Eye-Witness Watches as Huge Cat Attacks Deer. Two boxes, black with white printing,

9

presented selected quotes from the main article, but there were no pictures. I read the white-on-black quotes aloud: 'It was at least five foot long; there is no doubt in my mind about what I saw.' 'Visitors Heard Strange Noises Coming From Woods.'

Claire was still watching me expectantly. She gave a sharp little nod, as if to say 'Go on.' So I read the whole story to myself.

> A Corranbuie man claims he saw a black panther attack a red deer on Sunday night, and, in a totally separate incident in the same area, a visitor reports sighting a 'huge beast' after hearing strange noises in the woods.
>
> These eye-witness accounts come only two weeks after an Ardmartin householder claims to have driven off an attacking panther with his shotgun, and three months after the discovery near Mealdarroch of mutilated sheep carcasses raised the possibility that a 'big cat' might be living in Argyll.
>
> Mr Archie McFee, retired, was walking his dog about 10 p.m. on Sunday night when he was startled by the sight of a deer pursued by a black panther less than twenty feet in front of him.
>
> 'It all happened so quickly, but there is no doubt in my mind about what I saw. A red deer came crashing out of the woods, chased by a big black cat. It was the size of a tiger, at least five foot long not counting the tail. They both raced across the road in front of me and

then up into the woods on the other side, where I lost sight of them. I never believed those Big Cat stories until I saw it for myself.'

According to a neighbour of Mr McFee, visitors to her house last week reported unusual noises in the woods as well as a glimpse of some 'huge beast' which they were unable to identify.

Could there be a panther in our woods? Experts believe that a number of large cats such as panthers and pumas were released into the wild by their owners when the Dangerous Animals Act of 1976 required them to pay for a licence. Currently there is a government-sponsored hunt on for the 'Beast of Bodmin' reputed to roam Cornwall killing livestock. If such animals have managed to survive and reproduce and stay hidden in a relatively populous area such as Cornwall, how much more likely they would feel at home in the wilder parts of Scotland, where they could prey upon deer and other wild game in addition to livestock such as sheep.

Only time will tell if there's a panther in Argyll. The Editor of the Argyll Advocate *would be interested to hear from any readers who think they have evidence of its existence.*

Frightened, I turned to Claire.

'Is it true?'

'Why, Danni! Do you think the *Argyll Advocate* is the *Sunday Sport*? I don't make things up – I don't have to, not in exciting Argyll!'

'Does it attack people?'

'Only if they've had far, far too much to drink and happen to have been waving a shotgun around at four in the morning. Well, you have to tell the neighbours something.'

'Have you seen it?'

'It doesn't exist. There is no panther in Argyll – and not in Cornwall, either, no matter what they say. This is Britain, not Africa.'

'Then why print the story?'

'The story is true enough. There were some sheep killed, and there are people prepared to swear they saw a huge black beast which might have been a panther. Personally, I think Mr McFee forgot to put his glasses on when he went out walking the dog, and his neighbours and their visitors have over-active imaginations. As for the man in Ardmartin – pink elephants, my dear. If somebody says he's seen something, others soon start to see it, too. Human nature,' she sneered.

'But why print it? If there's no proof, and you don't believe them, why make a story out of it?'

'Because it's interesting. Because it gets people talking, and buying the paper. It's a bit of fun, that's all.'

I started to object that it seemed like lying to me, but then I shut up. It wasn't anything to do with me. Soon we were back on the road where I could lose myself in the wild empty spaces again.

It was a long way, nearly two hours drive to Claire's house. She lived just outside the tiny village of Dunmore, which was nothing more than a cluster of houses with a church and a public hall. The shops and the newspaper office were all in Mealdarroch, five miles away by road.

To me, the seaside had always meant Norfolk, where my Gran lived. It was flat sand or shingle beaches fronted by rows of well-kept bungalows and crawling with visitors in the summer.

Claire's seaside was very different, wild and rocky. Her house was tall and grey and stood all on its own, set well back from the single-track road and screened by a row of tall rhododendron bushes.

As she unlocked the heavy front door I heard animal sounds from inside: a low, threatening rumble, and then the scrape of claws against wood. Glimpsing black fur I shrank back, my heart pounding crazily, before I recognized the creature as an elderly black Labrador retriever.

It lurched at us out of the dimness of the hall with a muffled, half-swallowed bark.

'Hallo, Goofus,' said Claire. 'Danni, this is Goofy Gus. Gus, this is your new friend, Danni.'

I put out my hand for the dog to sniff and then I patted his head and stroked the soft, floppy ears.

'There should be another one around here somewhere. Gus, where's Lizzie?'

The dog tossed his head back and gave a bark. There was an answering bark from upstairs, and then the sound of a weight hitting the floor.

'On my bed again! Oh, Lizzie, you bad girl!' A younger, sleeker version of Gus appeared at the top of the stairs and began to bark.

'Oh, stop it,' Claire shouted. 'You're too late. As

13

a watchdog you are totally useless, Lizzie – totally! And you mustn't bark at Danni. She's our friend; she'll be staying with us. Come meet her.'

She came down the stairs and let me stroke her silky ears. I started to smile. I'd never been allowed to keep a pet as my dad's allergic to anything with fur or feathers. 'Want me to walk the dogs for you while I'm here?'

'I doubt you'll coax Gus out very far, but Lizzie will enjoy going on rambles with you. Out of the way, Goofus! Come on, I'll show you your room.'

My room was upstairs at the front of the house. I rushed to the window to look out. From up here I could see over the tops of the rhododendrons, over the road to the green pasture which sloped gently down to a strip of brown, stony shore and the edge of the grey-green, foaming sea. Towards the end of our journey it had started to rain, and it was still raining now, but a ray of sunlight lanced out of a cloud and made the wet air glitter.

'What's that out there? Is that an island?'

'Yes. It's the island of Jura. This house was called "Jura View" when I bought it, but I changed the name to *Fasgadh*.'

'What's that mean?'

'It's Gaelic for shelter or refuge. And that's what it's always been for me, a shelter from the world outside.'

I thought the world outside looked pretty wonderful, but I didn't say anything. There was a wind-twisted oak tree which looked climbable, but just a bit too far away to get to from my window. The bright green grass below looked thick and soft, but I wouldn't like to fall on it from up here.

'The bathroom is across the hall, and there's a shower-room downstairs if you prefer that.' Claire was going on about the details of my temporary home, but I didn't pay much attention, trying to work out how soon I could manage to get outside on my own for a good look around.

'We don't have to go out right away unless you want to; there's plenty of time for you to unpack and change and even have a bath if you like.'

'Go out?' I echoed.

'For dinner. I'm taking you to the Mealdarroch Inn to celebrate your arrival.'

My heart sank. 'Do I need to dress up?'

'Oh, no. You're fine. If you're hungry we can go now.'

I suddenly realized that I was hungry. The snack I'd been given on the plane seemed a long time ago. 'Let's go now.'

2

A Pair of Glowing Eyes

Mealdarroch was a pretty little village of white-painted houses set with their backs to the hills in a semi-circle around a small, sheltered harbour where nearly a dozen boats bobbed on the water. Claire parked on the harbour front and we walked across the road to the Mealdarroch Inn, which had a brightly-painted wooden sign showing a sailing ship in a harbour sheltered by an impossibly huge oak tree.

I expected a dining-room, but we went into the bar. I felt awkward, thinking Claire had forgotten my age and that we'd be kicked out (this had happened to me once with my father at home), but then I saw two little girls of about five and seven eating at a table with their parents, and on the far side of the room, huddled in a corner, was a group of boys who were maybe a couple of years older than me. They weren't eating, and they were all talking and laughing with drinks in their hands.

One of them looked up just then, as if he'd felt me watching, and caught my eye. He was the smallest of the lot, really skinny and raggedly dressed, with dark hair and something about his eyes that wouldn't let me look away.

Claire tugged me away. 'Over here, before some-one else takes the last table.'

'Your usual, madam?'

'Yes, thank you, Kevin. Danni, what would you like to drink?'

I looked at the man who was waiting for my order. He looked too old to be a waiter, and too badly-dressed. With his weather-beaten face and keen blue eyes he looked more like a sailor or a fisherman. 'I'll have a lemonade, please,' I said.

'One white wine, one lemonade,' he said, nodded, and went away.

Claire, meanwhile, was gazing around the room, nodding and smiling like a visiting royal.

'Do you know everybody here?' I asked.

'Oh, no, not this time of year. It's about half tourists, just now. I know that couple at the bar, and those two men, and . . . well, I'll probably intro-duce you to a few as the evening wears on.'

'Do you know those boys over in the corner, next to the fire?'

'Boys?' She sounded surprised; her eyes focused on them for the first time. 'Oh, yes, they're local. They're with Jamie. He's a teacher and he runs the sailing club – they're probably it, or part of it. They've probably been out sailing today, and he's brought them in here for a drink before they go home. Did you want to meet them? I suppose they're only a couple of years older than you, if that. I could ask Jamie . . .'

'That's OK,' I said hastily. 'I was just curious . . . anyway, the sailing club sounds fun. Do you think

17

I could join? I mean, I've never been sailing before, but I'd like to learn.'

'Well, we'll definitely teach you to sail while you're here, then. Now have a look at the menu.'

When Kevin came back with our drinks I still hadn't decided what I wanted to eat. 'The fish is always good,' he said, helpfully. 'And the smoked ham is a speciality.'

'I'll have the smoked ham salad,' I decided, handing him the menu.

'Certainly. A wise choice. And you, Madam? Will it be Madam's usual?'

Claire sighed heavily and rolled her eyes. 'Yes. I'm sorry . . .'

'Not at all, Madam. To serve you is my only desire.' He bowed and took the menus away.

I was laughing at his behaviour, which seemed so out of place here – calling Claire Madam and everything – when the look on her face stopped me cold. 'What?'

'Treating Kevin like a waiter!'

'Isn't he?'

'Of course not! He's my friend. He bought us drinks out of – didn't you realize he was joining us? That's his beer.'

For the first time I noticed that he'd set down three glasses on the table. I felt embarrassed, and then I got angry. 'Well, how was I supposed to know? You didn't tell me. You didn't even introduce him. If he's your friend—'

'Of course I introduced you!'

'No you didn't. Not properly.'

18

'Oh, never mind. It doesn't matter. He obviously thought it was funny.'

She was backing down because she knew she was wrong. I wasn't going to let her get away with it, but then a big, red-bearded man loomed over our little table.

'The return of the panther,' he intoned.

'Oh, have you seen it, too, Angus?' said Claire brightly. 'I'm always interested in eyewitness accounts.'

'What sort of eyewitness is Archie McFee? He's as blind as a bat.'

'Even if his eyesight is not what it once was, a countryman like Mr McFee is not going to mistake the way a deer moves for anything else – and from the shape of the head and the size of it, he's certain that what was chasing the deer had to be some sort of large cat. Others have seen it too, you know.'

'Oh, aye, in the middle of the night, after too much whisky. Kevin.'

'Angus.' The man I had mistaken for a waiter pulled out a stool and sat down beside me.

Angus put his hands flat on the table and leaned. 'I was saying to Claire, I canna believe this rubbish about some kind of tiger terrorizing the area.'

'It's not a question of belief,' said Claire. 'Either the beast exists or it doesn't. To find out which, we need evidence. We need more eyewitness accounts.'

'You won't be getting one from me,' he said. Then, grinning, he turned to look at me. 'How about this lassie? Would you not like to see a great wild beast in the woods? That would be something for your summer holidays, would it no? I expect your Auntie Claire would put a pretty picture of yourself on the front page if you said you'd seen the cat.'

I glared at him. 'Claire's not my auntie.' He went on grinning, and something in me snapped. 'I don't want my picture on the front page of the local rag, thanks very much. And I don't believe there's a wild panther out there any more than you do – any more than *she* does, never mind what she prints. Even if people did let some panthers lose in 1976 they'd all be dead now. How could animals that big survive and mate and raise their cubs without ever getting caught? I'm not stupid. I know they couldn't. There is no panther in Argyll.'

Angus leaned back as if the force of my anger was a strong wind that might knock him down. He whistled and shook his head. 'Well, she knows her mind and no mistake! Remind me never to ask you what you think of the Loch Ness Monster, lassie! Well, I'm off for my tea now. Evening to you all.'

Looking around I noticed that the thin, dark boy in the corner was watching me. Our eyes met again, and this time he smiled. It gave me a strange feeling, that smile, like he knew something about me. Seconds later he left his corner and walked away past me, out of the bar. He didn't even say goodbye to his friends. I stared after him, feeling confused and a little lost. I had the strongest urge to go after him, to make contact – although, if I did, I had no idea what I could say.

Kevin was asking me something, being friendly, drawing me in to the conversation. I made an effort to put the boy out of my head. After all, I thought, it was just a look, he was a stranger, that connection I imagined I'd felt couldn't have meant anything.

Kevin turned out to be the gamekeeper for a local estate. He kept track of the deer and other wild animals on the land, and took visitors out hunting.

As we ate our dinner the talk was about hunting, fishing, sailing, canoeing – all outdoor sports which I'd never really thought about before, but which were such a part of the local life. And they could be part of mine, at least for a little while. Kevin promised to take me sailing, and suggested that Claire could teach me to shoot.

I looked at her in surprise. 'You shoot?'

'Claire's a very good shot,' said Kevin. 'I took her stalking with me once, but she decided she didn't like hunting. So why she keeps guns, I don't know.'

'Hunting isn't my idea of fun,' said Claire. 'I could kill, if I had to. If my life depended on it. But I don't get any pleasure from killing deer or pheasants, and I really don't see why I should when there's a perfectly good butcher's shop in Meald-arroch.'

'All right,' said Kevin easily. 'Danni may feel differently . . .'

'I doubt it. Most girls her age are vegetarian, and even if they eat meat they can't bear the idea of killing little Bambis in the forest.'

I hate it when people assume they know all about

21

me because they know how old I am, or because I'm a girl, and quiet, and dress a certain way and seem to do what I'm told. You can't tell what a person's really like from what they are on the outside.

I said, 'I'd like to learn to shoot. Maybe I'd like hunting; how do I know till I try?'

Kevin grinned. 'That's the spirit.'

Claire still wore her cold fish face. 'I'll have to ask your parents how they feel about you handling a gun. If they say it's all right, I'll teach you to shoot.'

'And I'll teach you to hunt,' said Kevin.

When we came out of the inn it was late, but still daylight, and once we'd driven beyond the encircling shelter of the hills around Mealdarroch it was even lighter. The rain had stopped, the clouds had cleared away, and the sun was a vivid red ball hanging low over the sea.

From my side of the car I could look into an ancient, mysterious forest of oak, ash and beech, full of mossy dips and hollows and strangely-shaped rocks thrusting out of the soil. It made me think of an enchanted wood in a fairy tale. Staring into it, I moved into a sort of waking dream of running. It seemed I was loping along beside the car, running in an easy, tireless rhythm over a rise and then down into a hollow, until my eyes grew heavy and I felt the nearness of sleep. And then I realized I wasn't alone. There was another animal in the woods, running by my side.

My eyes jolted open. I stared hard out the

22

window. In the shadowy woods, something large and dark was moving.

'There's something out there,' I said.

'Probably a deer,' said Claire. She didn't take her eyes off the road ahead.

But I was sure it wasn't a deer. A deer didn't move like that; a deer was not that shape. It was too big, and the wrong colour, to be a fox. It could, perhaps, have been a very large dog, but somehow I didn't think it was.

The forest gave way to open, rocky heath, and now, as the animal continued to keep pace with the car and run alongside the road, I saw it, clear and unmistakeable. It was a huge, black cat, fully five feet long, with a tail more than half its length again. It was a black panther.

My heart seemed to stop with the wonder of the sight. As I stared, it looked back at me, and our eyes met. Its eyes were like twin glowing candles.

And then it turned, with a single, long, sinuous motion, and loped away over the hillside. I whipped around in my seat, desperate for another glimpse of it, but it was gone.

3

That Holiday Feeling

I woke the next morning with that special holiday feeling. At first it seemed totally quiet, but when I listened I could hear the sound of the sea, and a seagull calling. I jumped out of bed and rushed to the window.

As I looked out at the sun shining on the blue water I suddenly remembered the big black cat, and how it had looked at me with its golden eyes.

I shivered, remembering the intelligence, the meaning in its look. It had really *seen* me, looking past the surface, right through to the truth hidden in my soul.

But I must have imagined that. Maybe I'd dreamed the whole thing after so much talk about panthers.

I washed and dressed and went downstairs. Claire was in the kitchen, a too-warm room that smelled of dogs and coffee. From his place beside the Aga, Gus raised his head and thumped his tail in greeting, and the younger dog, Lizzie, came frisking over to greet me.

In a red dressing-gown, face bare of sunglasses or make-up, her hair rumpled, Claire looked different in the morning: softer and kinder.

I sat down at the table beside her and poured myself a glass of orange juice.

'Sleep well?'

'Yes, thank you.' I took a roll from the basket and spread it with butter.

'It's quiet here, isn't it? You'll find it a big change from the city. I hope you won't find it *too* quiet. It was just what I wanted when I came here, but you might not...'

'It's wonderful,' I said. 'I love it here.' I surprised myself a little, saying that, and saw that I had surprised her, too.

Her face relaxed into a pleased smile. 'Oh, good. I am glad... you never know if someone else will see it, feel things in the same way. I knew the moment I came to Argyll that I had to stay. It was like falling in love. I didn't ever want to leave, so I had to look about for a way of staying. I'd been working as a reporter down south, so when I heard there was a job opening for a newspaper editor, of course I applied. I don't know if I was better than any of the other applicants, but I was certainly the most determined. And I didn't see it as a temporary move, a way of getting experience before moving on – I knew I never wanted to move again.'

'So you left your old job just like that?'

'Well, no, actually I'd already left it. I'd – well, I'd had a spot of bother.' Her face had a pinched look; she'd tightened up again. I was sorry for that, but I was also curious.

'What do you mean?'

'Didn't your mother tell you? No? Well... it's a

long time ago, now. From another world. There was a man, where I worked. I never even went out with him except once, to tell him it was no go, but he decided he was in love with me. He became obsessed with me, he just wouldn't let me be. I left my job, but even that wasn't enough, he staked out my house . . .' She paused and, shaking, lit a cigarette. 'I'd written off to apply for various jobs, I knew I would have to leave Birmingham, but while I was waiting to hear the results, I went on holiday. I came to this part of Argyll by mistake, actually. I was on my way to the Highlands, and I took the wrong turning. And then I came to the sea, and I decided it didn't matter, nothing else mattered except finding a way of staying.'

'And you've never left?'

'I have to go to Glasgow occasionally. But I haven't been south of the border in years. But that's enough about me.' She sat up straight and stubbed out her cigarette. 'What would you like to do today?'

'Go to the beach.' I couldn't imagine beginning a holiday any other way – not, at least, when the sun was shining.

'Fine. There's a brilliant beach down at the point. I'll take you there, and then we can visit the castle.'

I'd been thinking about simply crossing the road, but Claire drove down to the end of the little peninsula on which she lived. The road ended there, but she told me that if we clambered around the rocky headland we'd come upon an old, unpaved track which led to Mealdarroch. On that side, the sea was

26

called Loch Ban. On this side, it was the Sound of Jura.

It was the most beautiful beach I'd ever seen, curving, broad and white, clean and practically empty. Besides us, there were only four or five small children being looked after by two women at the far end of the beach. Occasionally the wind carried fragments of their tiny voices to us, less distracting than the cry of a gull skimming low over the water. There were no sunbathers or windsurfers, no one selling ice-creams or setting out beach chairs. I couldn't believe no one else knew about this place.

But there was one drawback, which I discovered as soon as I waded into the water. It was *freezing*. And the wind was unrelenting.

'Does it ever get warmer?' I asked.

Claire shook her head. 'I haven't been sea-bathing in years. The children around here all go in, but not the visitors. I think you have to be born to it, maybe be part seal.'

'Sure, that would help.'

'People used to believe it. All along the coast they still tell stories about people who married one of the seal-folk. There are families who can trace their line of descent back to a particular man or woman who came from the sea only a few generations back.'

'Granny was a seal?' I remembered stories I'd read about animals who took off their fur coats to reveal the human inside, and I remembered how uneasy zoos made me feel. I hadn't been very often – the first time I'd come face to face with an animal in a cage it had given me a very weird feeling. Not just pity for a wild thing caged; I'd felt as if it knew something about me that I didn't know myself. As if it could tell me something, if I only knew how to listen. And suddenly I was remembering the panther, how its eyes had burned into mine.

'You're cold,' said Claire.

'I'm all right.'

'No you're not. Come on, let's go back to the car. We'll go somewhere else. . . . We could go to look at the seals.'

'Where?'

'*Eilean nan Ron*. The name means the Island of the Seals, but it's not really an island, just a group of rocks in Loch Ban. It's more sheltered on that side. The seals go there to pup in the spring, and then lie about in the sun all day.'

Not seals in an enclosure, then. I felt relieved. 'That sounds nice.'

The seals, adults and pups together, were sunning themselves on various of the half-dozen large rocks that thrust up from the sea-loch a mile or so from Mealdarroch, sharing the space with cormorants and seagulls. I shielded my eyes against the sun and stared across the water at them. 'What would happen if somebody went out to the rocks? Would the seals all swim away?'

'They might. They might just wait to see what you were there for. Seals are very curious about us. I'll never forget the time I had a dozen of them clustered around the sides of my boat while I sang to them.'

I could hardly believe my ears. 'You sang to them?'

'Yes.'

'Why?'

I couldn't read the expression that flickered across her face. It might have been sadness. 'Well, I just had a feeling they might like it. According to the legends, seals love music. And they certainly did seem to respond . . . Oh, I don't know. It was a long time ago. I was a little bit fey, a little bit crazy, more romantic then. I wanted to believe in magic.'

'Seals aren't magic.'

'That's right. Seals are only animals. And if they responded to my singing, it wouldn't mean there was a connection between us, or that they understood me in a way that – that's all I meant by magic. Magical thinking. Wishful thinking. I wanted to believe I had some special connection with animals. And seals are so particularly appealing somehow. I felt, if I could make contact . . .' she broke off, folding her lips together tightly and shaking her head.

I felt sorry for her, but also excited. She sounded much more like the Claire I had imagined from long ago. Hoping for more, I said, 'Maybe you do have a special talent for communicating with animals – some people do.'

She shook her head. 'You're young. When you're older you'll understand. Even if we could talk with animals, we mustn't – not any more. We've left all that behind us. We're not animals any more – at least, we're not only that. Humans are the only animals who can make the choice *not* to be, not

29

to act on instinct, but to change ourselves, to be civilized.'

'But you don't have to *be* an animal to understand them and like them.'

'I'm not talking about keeping pets, Danni. I mean something much more – Oh, just forget it.' She gave her head a tight, irritated shake. 'You're not old enough to understand. Maybe you'll never have to. Enjoy your innocence while you can. Come on, I'll take you to see the castle now.'

I was annoyed by the way she used my age as an excuse not to give me a proper argument, and I hadn't finished watching the seals. I didn't say anything more then, but I didn't forget that conversation.

The next morning we went to church in Dunmore, and Kevin Clark came back with us to Fasgadh for lunch – which he cooked. Watching him frying sausages, potatoes and onions, I wondered about his relationship with Claire. They didn't kiss or seem romantic, but they obviously knew each other well, and seemed closer than just friends.

After lunch we went over to Kevin's boat in Mealdarroch harbour. I'd never been sailing before.

'We'll make a sailor of you by tea-time,' Kevin promised.

I wasn't sure, but he was, and he had me handling the tiller before I really knew what it was. It was fun, but I was just as happy when Claire took over. So was the boat: it sprang forward, practically flying out of the harbour under her hand.

Now that I could relax, I gazed across the water

where the brown and green hills were like crouching animals, and then looked around. We were approaching Eilean nan Ron, and the rocks were covered with the softly-furred, blobby bodies of seals just as they had been the day before.

But now we were so much closer. I could see the big liquid eyes, the sprouting whiskers, on even the smallest babies, and my heart beat hard with excitement.

All of a sudden one seal launched itself off the rock into the water and there was a subdued splash. Two more small splashes followed, and another seal gave a brief, grunting bark.

Rounded, earless, blunt-nosed, whiskery heads, shining wet, popped out of the water, one on either side of the boat. They looked mild and interested, friendly, slightly comical, absolutely charming. I felt suddenly on the verge of tears without knowing why, and I leaned over the side to see them better.

With a painfully tight grip on my arm, Claire hauled me back. 'Don't do it!'

'What?' I felt dazed, as if she'd woken me, and I was bewildered. 'I wasn't doing anything!'

'You were practically in the water.'

'They're wild animals,' said Kevin. 'You can't pet them. If one of them thought you were threatening, they might bite.'

'Please let go. You're hurting my arm.'

'Not until you promise me.'

'Promise what? I won't pat them!'

'That you won't jump in.'

'Of course I won't!'

31

'I saw the way you were looking at them.' She let go my arm, but kept her face close to mine. In a low voice she said, 'I know how it feels. You have to fight it!'

I scowled at her and rubbed my arm, making a show of it. I felt scared and I didn't want her to see. 'I don't know what you're talking about.'

'Coming about,' said Kevin, and there was a brief flurry of activity. By the time it was over, we were in different places, and Claire was gazing into the distance as if nothing had happened. I didn't want to stir things up, so I didn't say anything, but I watched her warily for a long time.

4

Exploring

Claire offered to take me into Mealdarroch with her when she went to work the next day, but she wasn't bothered when I said I'd rather stay behind.

'Sure you won't be lonely?'

'Lizzie will come with me, won't you, girl?' She licked the hand I put out to her. 'I want to go exploring,' I said. 'That's all right, isn't it?'

She nodded. 'Just use common sense. Of course you mustn't go swimming, or out on the water by yourself.'

'I wanted to go into the hills.'

'Well, take a waterproof, in case the weather changes, and a map and a compass. I can give you a rucksack to carry all the things you should have – I'd take some food and a bottle of water, and insect repellent.'

I thought about harnessing Lizzie to carry the essential supplies. It was beginning to seem like a major expedition, with me playing the overdressed Victorian explorer when what I really wanted to do was go native.

But as soon as I was out of the house, breathing in the sea air, I got that hopeful, holiday feeling again, and nothing else mattered. Lizzie had looked so miserable when I fastened the lead to her collar that I took it off again immediately. She pranced happily at my side.

I felt we'd both been let off the lead. At home, I had to give my parents a detailed travel plan whenever I left the house: where I was going, by what route, how long it would take me to get there, and when I'd be back. I couldn't imagine my mother ever letting me go out for a whole day, just exploring. But things must be different here, so far from the dangers of the city.

It was a still, warm, overcast day. We walked along the road a little way, meeting no one, hearing nothing but birds, some sort of buzzing insects in the grass, and the soft shushing sound of the sea on my right. Then I caught sight of a rough, half-overgrown track on the left, leading up into the hills, and my heart beat faster.

'This way,' I called to Lizzie. Leaving the paved road, we entered another world.

The bracken that lined the track grew higher than my head, huge green fronds like something from the age of dinosaurs. Sheltered from sea-breezes, it was even warmer here, moist and steaming gently. There was a thick, rich, green smell with something faintly rank lurking underneath – and there were flies. I began to walk faster, almost running, to get away from them.

For a little while the track went uphill, but then it began to descend. I heard the sound of rushing water, and a short while later glimpsed a fast-flowing, rocky stream – a burn they called it here. The path followed the course of the water for some way, across scrubby, open heath. Brambles snaked across the path, but none of the berries I saw were anywhere near ripe.

Up ahead I saw a house. I stopped, confused and disappointed. I'd been enjoying the feeling of wilderness so much that it hadn't occurred to me this half-overgrown track might take me back to civilization. Then I realized that the building had no roof. It was a ruin. Going closer to investigate, I saw three or four other ruined buildings close by. There was very little left of most of them, just crumbling walls and one nearly intact chimney stack. Had this been a village once upon a time, or only a farm? I remembered the Ordnance Survey map Claire had given me, and decided to stop and find out if the ruin was marked on it.

I had just shrugged off my rucksack when I felt them: a crawling, buzzing sensation on my face. I blinked and waved my hands, wondering where this cloud of dust had come from, and then I realized what it really was: a storm of tiny, biting insects. Midges.

Claire had made a joke about them: the defenders of the Highlands. But they were no joke. I could feel them inside my mouth and crawling up my nose. I started spitting, and then, tossing my head, began to run like a crazy person. Lizzie barked and ran after me.

Travelling uphill seemed like a good strategy. Claire had told me midges preferred low, wet, sheltered spots. Wind would blow them away, and they didn't survive well in strong sunlight, either.

Unfortunately, the weather favoured midges that day. There was hardly a breath of wind, and no ray of sunshine penetrated the cloud cover. They weren't too bad as long as I kept moving, and the insect repellent I'd put on earlier did help, but I never escaped them entirely.

I paused for a drink of water and to refresh my midge-proofing. Lizzie sat down and panted and gazed at me hopefully. When I didn't give her what she wanted she trotted off – I assumed to drink from the burn, which I could still hear, although it was out of sight.

I was alone. Probably, I thought, as I looked around me, at the lowering sky and the rocky, scrubby hillside, more alone than I'd ever been before in my life. The nearest human beings must be miles away, and there was no one in the whole world who knew exactly where I was at that moment. It was a great feeling.

And then my skin prickled and I knew, with absolute, instinctive certainty, that I wasn't alone.

Someone, or something, was watching me.

I looked around sharply. There were plenty of hiding places: a bristling gorse-bush, a jutting rock, the bracken.

I jumped to my feet and called for Lizzie. At first my voice came out as a squeak, but then grew stronger.

Something black, moving very fast, was a blur at

the edge of my sight; I whirled around, and there was Lizzie.

'Good girl! Good dog!' I was almost crying, so happy to see her again, so relieved that I was not alone. But as I patted her I felt her stiffen, and her head came up and her nose worked away at some scent she caught on the air. Then, with a low and dangerous growl, she ran off in pursuit.

'Lizzie! No! Come back!'

I gazed after her, helpless, and saw something large and black – the fur as absolutely black as Lizzie's own – streak between one concealing clump of gorse and another. Definitely an animal – could Gus have got out?

But if Lizzie had caught Gus's scent she would have been welcoming, she wouldn't have growled and taken off like that.

It was the panther; I felt absolutely sure of it. Had Lizzie scared it off, or would it turn on her, attack and kill her – and then maybe come back and kill me?

I shuddered, and clenched my teeth together. More than anything, more than frightened, I felt furious with that animal for spoiling everything, for making me frightened and taking away my freedom. But there was no way I could go on sitting there like a stupid decoy, waiting for what it would do. I would have to head back to Fasgadh.

The midges were awful – I kept walking into clinging clouds of them. The air seemed impossibly still and heavy, but I only realized why when it began to rain.

It absolutely poured down, and there was nowhere to shelter. I struggled with the rucksack and finally got out the folded mac, but by the time I managed to put it on I was so wet there didn't seem much point. I fastened it anyway, and trudged away down the hill.

Time passed and the rain slackened and I was still walking. I had expected to reach the ruined buildings by now, but instead I was in a wood I hadn't seen before. I must have come down the hill by a different route without realizing. And I hadn't seen the burn at all, although I thought it must be close by.

I stood very still and didn't even shake my head against the midges as I listened for the sound of rushing water. All I could hear was the irregular drips and splatters of rain on leaves.

There was no path, no obvious way to go. I moved to the left, thinking that I would follow the burn, which must eventually come out in the sea, but then I stopped again, realizing that I didn't actually know where the burn was. I had been travelling, I thought, pretty steadily in one direction, but the problem was, I didn't know *which* direction.

Then I thought of the compass.

Raindrops dripped and splashed onto the folded map as I turned the nylon rucksack inside out in desperation. There was the half-empty water-bottle and the sandwich I hadn't eaten, but nothing else. No insect repellent. No compass.

They had fallen out somewhere and I hadn't noticed. I was lost.

Luckily I realized I was starting to panic and managed to calm myself. I wasn't in the Gobi desert, after all. I couldn't be more than a few miles from Dunmore, and I still had the map.

I unfolded the damp paper carefully. The rain, which seemed to have stopped, began to pelt down harder. But what bothered me the most, what made it impossible to concentrate on reading the map, was the feeling that I was being watched.

My skin crawled. It was even worse this time, because now I thought I knew what was watching me, and there was no Lizzie to chase it off.

But maybe it didn't know that. I had to do something. Screaming seemed too stupid, and running might be fatal. So, making my voice as strong and sure as I could, I called for a dog who wasn't there.

'Lizzie! Come here, girl!'

The undergrowth rustled as something moved towards me.

With my heart in my throat, I whirled around to face it. But there, instead of the beast I'd expected, was a boy.

He was as wet as if he'd been swimming. His black hair was plastered flat against his head, and I could practically count his ribs beneath the once-white T-shirt which clung like a second skin to his skinny chest. He smiled, and I realized I'd seen him before.

'You were in the bar, in the Mealdarroch Inn on Friday night!'

'Oh, aye. And you're the girl doesn't believe in our panther.'

So he had heard. And, what was worse, remembered. I hoped I wasn't blushing. 'Didn't you ever say something you didn't mean just to get at somebody?'

He raised his eyebrows and shrugged.

'I wasn't talking to you, anyway.'

'Well, excuse *me*.'

If I hadn't been blushing before, I surely was by then. Couldn't I open my mouth around him without putting my foot in it? 'I didn't mean it like that. It was just . . . the whole thing was a stupid conversation that I didn't want to be in so I . . . made it worse, I suppose. It's not important now.'

'No?'

Why couldn't he leave it? 'Was that your sailing club?'

'Sailing club?'

'Do you like to sail?'

He just stared at me, as if I'd said something that made no sense. I began to get annoyed. 'You're awfully wet.'

'Aye, and you're dry as a bone.'

I had to laugh, then. It had been a stupid thing to say. 'Oh, yes, raindrops bounce off my special, invisible force-field.' I had to stop because I was laughing too hard to say more.

He stared at me, bemused. What could he have thought? I couldn't stop laughing. I sank down on my heels in the wet forest in the middle of a shower of rain and I howled with laughter.

At least, I thought I was laughing, until I felt his hands on my shoulders as he crouched beside me, and then I realized my face was wet not only with rain but with tears. My chest ached.

'What's the matter?'

Everything, I thought. I struggled to catch my breath. Nothing seemed funny any more. I sniffed and wiped at my wet face with the back of my equally wet hand. 'I'm lost.'

He shook his head.

'Yes I am! I don't know where I am.'

'Where do you want to be?'

That nearly started me crying again. I shook my head.

'It's all right,' he said. 'I know these woods. I couldn't get lost around here if I tried.'

'Do you know Fasgadh?'

He looked blank.

'It's where I'm staying. Claire Tinker's house, by Dunmore.'

'Oh, aye, I know the house you mean. Will I take you there?'

'Please.' I followed him, but he didn't go in either of the directions I would have chosen, and after a few minutes of silent walking I began to worry about where he was taking me. 'Shouldn't we have come to the road by now?'

'We're not going by the road. This is my way.' He gave me a sly, sideways smile. 'You can go your own way if you'd rather.'

'I told you, I—'

'Ssssh. What's Claire Tinker to you? A relation?'

'Not really. Well, she's my godmother.'

'Your mum kick you out, then?'

'Of course not! I'm only here for the holidays.'

'So where's she gone for hers?'

'She's not on holiday. She had to go to New York, to work. My dad's at home, but he's working, too, so he's not around much. It wouldn't have been much fun for me to stay there, so they fixed it up for me to come here.'

'And you get to go home again at the end of the summer.'

'Yes, sure.'

'I thought maybe you were like me. My parents didn't want me. I thought maybe you were the same.'

I knew he wouldn't want sympathy, especially not from a stranger, so I swallowed all the sorries I might have said. 'What happened?'

'My dad left just after I was born. I don't remember him. My mum's new boyfriend didn't want to be lumbered with a kiddie, so she parked me with her sister, my Auntie Jean, when I was about four, and went off somewhere. I never saw her again. I thought I'd stay with Auntie Jean for ever, but three years ago her new boyfriend got fed up and threw me out.'

That really shocked me. 'But they can't do that! People can't just throw their children out like that!'

'Oh, no? Anyway, I wasn't theirs. I would've been taken into care, I think, except by then, luckily, I'd met the old man, so I knew – well, he taught me – a thing or two. How to take care of myself. We came up here, then, right away from anybody that would have known me, so that was all right. I stay with him, and I go to school regular, and that keeps the social services off me. I do all right.' Then he stopped and made a gesture. 'Know where you are now?'

I looked and saw, first, the blue-grey glitter of the sea on the horizon, and then, closer at hand, the solid bulk of Fasgadh.

We were on the hillside behind the house, and I could see a path running down to the garden fence. 'Oh! Thank you. Do you want to come with me? You could dry off a bit, and we could have something to eat.'

He was shaking his head before I'd finished.

'Claire's not there,' I said, in case that was what he minded. 'She won't be back until five.'

'But her dogs are. Dogs and I don't get along.'

Following his gaze, I saw that Lizzie had got home ahead of me. She was waiting patiently by the back door for some kind person to come along and let her in. 'They wouldn't hurt a fly, they're really friendly dogs. But I could put them in the kennel if you—'

'I won't come with you just now. Will I see you again?'

'Sure. How about tomorrow? Now you know where I live—'

'We'll meet somewhere else. Do you know the dun?'

'What's that?'

'On top of the hill there's an old dun – a hill-fort.'

I looked where he was pointing. 'How do I find it?'

'Do you not see it? That pile of rocks on top? Well, anyway, this path will take you up through the woods, all the way to the top of the hill. It's quite easy, only a bit of a climb right at the end. You'll like it, the dun; it's one of my best places.'

'OK. I'll see you there tomorrow morning.'

5

Fin

It was only when I tried to tell Claire about my new friend that I realized I knew nothing about him.

'You didn't ask him his name?'

'It didn't seem important. He didn't ask me mine, either. It was like we already knew each other. Well, in a way we had already met.'

She gave me a hard look. 'When?'

'He was in the bar, in Mealdarroch, where we went for dinner. Remember? I asked you about him then. You didn't know him, but you knew the man he was with. You said he must be part of the sailing club.'

She relaxed. 'Oh, one of Jamie's boys! Well, I'm glad you've made a friend; it'll be more fun for you. Do try to remember to ask him his name when you see him again, won't you?'

There was a sagging wire fence around the garden, but it was less a barrier than a boundary-marker, and I had no trouble climbing over it into the woods.

Already I felt at home here; leaving the house was like escaping into myself. I thought of a bird leaving a cage for the open air, a fish slipping out of a net and back into the sea. I didn't even think about the panther and how frightened I'd been the day before; my thoughts rushed ahead to the boy who was waiting for me. With him at my side I wouldn't get lost and I wouldn't panic.

It was funny, the way I'd felt drawn to him the very first time I saw him, almost as if I'd recognized a relation in a crowd of strangers. Nothing like that had ever happened to me before, yet it seemed perfectly natural. It was as if something connected us before we met, drawing us together so that we *had* to meet.

The trail rose, and the woods went from being a mixture to rows of conifers rising so high their heavy, green-needled branches blocked out the sun. It was dark and cool and quiet, like being at the bottom of a canyon. The ground was carpeted with green moss which was soft and springy underfoot, easy walking.

Then the path emerged from the woods and the slope grew steeper. Coming out into sunlight and the peppery smell of gorse, I had to use my hands as well as my feet to get to the top.

There it was before me, a heap of grey rocks. Out of the heap grew a single long foxglove, waving slightly in the breeze like a solitary pink flag. Then, beyond the cairn, I saw a dry-stone wall, maybe two metres high. As I picked my way towards it I realized it was bigger than I'd first thought, the remains of what had once been a sizeable circular enclosure. I wondered what sort of people had lived here, and when it had finally been abandoned.

'Hiya.'

His voice made me start and almost lose my footing. I clutched at a nearby rock and looked around. He was high above me, perched on the wall.

'Come on around and climb up from the inside.'

The wall dwindled away to lumpy rubble; I picked my way over fallen stones until I was 'inside' – a stony hollow within the embrace of a crumbling semi-circle of wall. There was a great view down the steep hillside, away to Loch Ban. I saw the white houses of Mealdarroch winking in the sun.

The boy leaped down and landed lightly, without stumbling, beside me. 'Welcome to *Dun a'Choin Duibh*.'

'What?'

'Gaelic for the Fort of the Black Dog.'

I smiled, thinking of Lizzie and Gus. 'Wonder if Claire knows that?' That reminded me of another question. 'What's *your* name?'

He looked wary, and I saw I'd put my foot in it again. I said quickly, 'It's just it seems odd not knowing. I don't know why I didn't introduce myself yesterday. I'm Danni Arnott.'

'Names aren't important.'

I shrugged. 'But they're useful. Even this place has a name.'

'Just about every place does, if you look on the map.' He relaxed, considering this. 'Not that the names make any difference – most people don't even know them. Or if they know them, they don't know what they mean.'

'But you do.'

'Aye, well, it interests me, I don't know why. Lots of things do that aren't any use. The old man doesn't understand why I want to know so many useless things, why I want to keep on at school and that, but.' He looked straight at me, no longer mistrustful. 'I'm Fin.'

'Just Fin?'

'Aye. That's *my* name. In Mealdarroch, for school and that, they have me down as Finlay Black. That's because the old man calls himself Malcolm Black. It's easier, see, if we have the same name, then they can think he's my dad, or my granddad. I don't know what my real dad's name was. Could've been Black, for all I know, but probably wasn't. But Black's good enough, a good enough name for me to use.'

'Is that why you like this place? Because of the name?' As I asked, I realized it was a stupid question. Even if he liked it for 'black' he wouldn't like it for 'dogs'.

He laughed. 'Ah, no, man, you want to know why I like this place? Look around!' He flung out his arms, inviting me to share the view. There were the forested hills and Loch Ban in one direction, and in the other, the sea, with the mountains of Jura painted on the horizon. We stood in silence for awhile, until I asked him about the fort.

'Oh, it's been here probably two thousand years. Nobody really knows. Very few duns have been properly excavated, so most of what's been written about them is guesswork. They don't know if people would have lived here all the time, or just come up here with their cattle to be safe from raiders now and again. Let me show you something.'

We went up and over the wall. On the other side there was a doorway which opened onto a passage leading under the wall. I followed him, but as soon as we were inside the close, dark, underground space I wished I hadn't. There was a strange, musky odour which overlaid the more usual smells of damp and earth. I didn't know what it was, but it made the hairs stand up all over my body. Whether it was the smell of the confined space I didn't know, but something made me desperately, frantically nervous. I had to get out.

'I'm going,' I said.

He followed me back to the surface and watched as I gulped at the clean, open air. 'What's wrong?'

As the pounding of my heart died down I started to feel embarrassed. 'Sorry. I just suddenly felt . . . I don't know . . . in danger. I didn't belong in there. That smell—' I was sure suddenly that it had been an animal smell. 'Do you think it could be some animal's home? I don't know what . . . a badger, or a fox's den, maybe?'

'It's my den.'

'Do you go there a lot?' The idea was creepy.

He didn't answer. He could see what I thought of his special place. To change the subject I rummaged in my rucksack. 'Want something to eat? I brought some sandwiches.'

His eyes lit up when he saw the food, so we had a picnic perched on the crumbling walls of the ancient hill-fort. When he'd finished the water in the bottle he offered to refill it for me.

'Where?'

'Yon burn.'

'You can drink the water straight from the burn?'

He smiled at my ignorance. 'Where do you think the water in Mrs Tinker's taps comes from?'

'But doesn't it have to be processed or something first?'

'That's only when there's something wrong with the water. But if there's nothing in it to harm you, apart from the odd dead wee frog . . .'

'Oh, I don't know, I expect the frog gives it a bit of flavour!'

'Aye, it does, and all.'

We grinned at each other. I put my face up and shut my eyes to feel the sun, purely happy.

The rest of the day I spent with him, and the next few days after that, exploring the land. I'd take the dogs out for a quick run, and then I'd leave them in the house or lock them in the kennel, and then, with a packed lunch big enough for two in my rucksack, I'd take the path up to the dun. It was soon as familiar to me as the route to the corner shop back home.

Fin was always there before me, no matter how early I started out. Although it seemed to me an area too vast to cover in a year, he knew the wilderness for miles round about Fasgadh as if it were his own small garden. He hadn't been born here; he'd been in Argyll for only the past three years. He must have done almost nothing else but explore the countryside, I thought, and I felt some pity for his lonely, solitary existence until I realized the land was such a good friend to him he hardly needed any other.

He taught me how to look and how to see, how to listen, and understand what I heard. Following him, I learned to walk lightly on my feet. Hidden by the bracken and gorse, or resting on a springy bed of heather, we spied on the red deer, and once spotted a badger in its holt. A golden eagle flew overhead; he told me he had seen where it nested.

One afternoon we gorged ourselves on wild raspberries, stripping the canes of their soft fruit and eating until our mouths, hands and clothes were all blotched and stained with red. He pointed out edible mushrooms, and encouraged me to pick them. But the handfuls I gathered were soon bruised and withered in the bottom of my rucksack, and when I showed Claire my treasures, hoping she would want to cook them, she wrinkled her nose and made me chuck them out.

We didn't talk very much, Fin and I. We didn't seem to need a lot of words between us. If I tried to find out more about Fin's life, he withdrew, so I never pressed it.

Once he asked if I was really going to leave Argyll at the end of August. What if my mother decided to stay in New York? Would I go to that far-away foreign city, too?

Then it was my turn to withdraw. I told him shortly that my mother and I would both be back home in Birmingham by the end of the summer. I knew he wanted it to happen, he wanted me to stay and be like him: wild, motherless and free. And I was worried because it didn't seem completely impossible. In her phone calls, my mother was alarmingly enthusiastic about New York and the work she was doing there. She'd dropped one or two hints about the possibility of future jobs there, and how much America had to offer, and wouldn't I enjoy a visit some time? I was sure I wouldn't. The whole idea of New York scared me; I didn't even want to think about it. So I told her about my new-found love of the countryside. A little to my surprise, my enthusiasm pleased her. My Dad, too, was enthusiastic about my explorations, and about my learning to sail. He thought I should take up fishing as well, and was in favour of my learning to shoot. From the way he talked, you'd have thought I had months or even years ahead of me in Scotland to acquire these new skills instead of only a few weeks. Both of them said, more than once, how pleased and relieved they were that I was happy and had settled in so quickly. Somehow, I didn't like hearing that – I wanted them to miss me, and say so. But I couldn't deny that I was in the middle of the best holiday I'd ever had.

And then I saw the panther again.

I'd come back to Fasgadh a little later than usual

that evening. I'd stopped wearing my watch because I didn't want to break it and because I didn't need it when Fin was so good at judging the time of day from the way the sky looked, even when it was cloudy.

But on that day I got back to find the dogs in the house, where they greeted me with affectionate whines and tail-thumping, and a note from Claire telling me I'd missed my chance of sharing a meal with her in the Mealdarroch Inn. Because I'd stayed out so late I'd have to make do with whatever I could scrounge in the kitchen.

I didn't mind; in fact, I was relieved to have escaped the dinner she thought was such a treat. I went upstairs to have a wash, and I'd just reached my room when I heard the dogs begin to bark hysterically.

Something moving on the lawn caught my eye at the window; something dark and out of place. For a moment I thought one of the dogs had got out, but when I stopped and looked I saw it was the panther.

It wasn't passing through. It was standing still, watching the house, and it was in plain sight, as if it didn't have to hide. It was letting itself be seen, just as it had done when it ran alongside the car on my first night here.

Fear chilled me. Why? Why was it here? Why did it want to see me, and be seen? I dropped into a crouch and crab-walked away from the window, out of view. As I did, I noticed my camera on the

53

table, and then a different sort of excitement made me shiver.

I could take a picture. I could prove the panther existed. No more arguing over eye-witness accounts: I'd have evidence to wave under Claire's nose.

The camera was in my hands, and there were six exposures left on the film.

I crept cautiously back to the window. I was worried about the light, because the sun was so low, and about taking a picture through glass, but I had to try. As I steadied myself against the window-ledge and raised the camera to my eye I concentrated on getting the animal in frame. It seemed to be waiting for me, standing perfectly still.

I pressed the shutter and a red light blinked a warning; I pressed again, more firmly, and heard the click.

The great cat's head came up. Surely it couldn't have heard such a tiny sound? The golden eyes started into my own.

I felt dizzy. I couldn't move. Things seemed to be moving around me, and I thought I heard a voice, speaking urgently, telling me something vital, but it spoke a language I couldn't understand.

The panther turned its head and leaped away.

In nervous reflex my finger came down on the shutter and fired off another shot. And then another. The panther was loping away from me now, but I kept shooting until the film was finished and the animal had vanished behind the rhododendrons.

6

The Camera Never Lies

First thing next morning I gave Claire the roll of film and asked if she could get it developed.

'We can drop it off in Oban,' she said.

That one little word, 'we' made my heart sink. 'Do I have to go too?'

She looked hurt as she tried to laugh. 'It's meant to be a treat, not a chore! I have to do the shopping, but you could stay at the swimming pool if you'd like.'

'Oh, thanks, that sounds nice,' I said. Now I felt guilty. I'd lost track of the days; I'd forgotten this was Saturday, when Claire didn't work, and we always went somewhere together. 'It's just that I'd told Fin I'd meet him.'

'Well, call and tell him you can't. I'm sure he'll understand. Or, no, I've a better idea. Why not invite him along? It would be a treat for him, and I'll finally get a chance to meet this mysterious friend of yours. It's high time I did.' There was an edge to her smile that made me nervous. It wasn't that I didn't want them to meet, but Fin was as self-willed as she was. At her request, I'd invited him to dinner twice already, but he simply refused to come.

'I can't call him – I don't have his number.'

'Oh, of course, they're not on the phone. I'll tell you what: we can stop by his place on our way to Oban. What's wrong?'

'I don't know where he lives.'

She smiled. 'You don't, but I do. I've been asking around about your new friend – after all, you're my responsibility. Your mother would want to know something about anyone you were spending so much time with. It's not hard to find out about people around here.

'Your friend lives with his grandfather, Malcolm Black. They're not from these parts; they turned up about three years ago. But they haven't really settled in; they keep to themselves, I heard. Old Mr Black did some work for Bruce McVay, he's a farmer, and Bruce let them stay in a caravan he had on his land. I think Bruce may regret this now, because the old man has become less and less reliable. He disappears for days at a time, so Bruce doesn't get much work out of him, but he doesn't like to turf them out, not with the boy. No one has a bad thing to say about the boy, I was glad to learn. One of his teachers is a friend of mine, and she says he's a good student and has never been in any trouble that she knows of, but she worries that he's not looked after properly at home.'

It was horrible to hear all this about Fin's life. I could imagine how he'd hate it if he knew there was a network of spies reporting and speculating on his personal life.

'All right,' I said, to stop her. 'You know where

he lives, let's go there. We'd better hurry, or we'll miss him.'

In fact, I was sure he must be on his way to the dun, if he was not there already. It was pointless to go to his house to tell him I wouldn't be able to meet him, but I didn't tell Claire. It was better to let her have her own way.

Fin lived farther away than I'd imagined – farther than I'd have thought possible, on the other side of Mealdarroch. It took nearly twenty minutes to drive there. How, I wondered, did he manage to get to the dun so early every day?

The first thing that came to mind when I saw Fin's home was: no wonder he likes the dun.

It wasn't a modern, posh, all-mod-cons sort of caravan, but an ancient, battered tin box which appeared to have been dropped into a rocky field, facing the wild ocean. It didn't look like a place where anyone could live.

'Heaven help them during the winter gales,' said Claire, pulling off the road to park on the narrow shoulder. 'Although, believe it or not, that caravan's been stuck there for as long as I can remember and doesn't look much the worse for wear. If it wasn't blown away two years ago maybe it never will be.'

'Did someone live there before Fin and his old man?'

'Oh, no. Bruce used it for his relatives in the summer. Maybe he let it out to campers occasionally, but I think it would have to be a pretty desperate camper to stay for more than one night.'

'Can't they find anywhere else to live?' I asked. 'Couldn't they get a council flat?'

'From what I've heard, old Mr Black would never ask for one. He's a man who keeps himself to himself, as they say. He doesn't ask any favours. And there's no saying what they left behind when they came here – it's hard to believe this could be an improvement over anything, but maybe it was.'

'I'll just run up and check if he's in,' I said. The caravan looked uninhabited; I was sure there was no one in.

'I'll come with you.'

'You don't have to.'

'I'll come with you.'

So we both trudged across the muddy field, Claire fastidiously picking her way in white sandals and wincing whenever she made a bad choice about where to step.

I knocked at the door and it opened.

A short, white-haired, whiskery man with bloodshot eyes stood there, glaring at us like an evil dwarf out of a fairy-tale. He wore a dirty, once-white vest and baggy brown trousers held up with a bit of cord, and he looked ill and dangerous. There was a smell, sour and rank, that came from him or the interior of the caravan; whatever it was made my stomach lurch and my heart pound harder with dread. I shrank away from him. My skin was crawling as though it wanted to run away on its own. I forced myself to stand still.

Claire sounded astonishingly bright and sociable when she spoke, as if she hadn't noticed a thing wrong. 'Hello! You must be Mr Black. I'm Claire Tinker, and this is my god-daughter, Danni. We were looking for young Finlay – is he about?'

He stared at us with his jaw thrust forward. Just as I was beginning to think he hadn't understood what she'd said, he shook his head.

'He's not? Oh, what a pity. Danni was meant to be meeting him, and she just called round to tell him she couldn't make it today. I hope you'll pass on her apologies to him.'

His eyes shifted from Claire to me and back again. I felt in terrible danger. Finally he said, in a low voice that sounded rusty from disuse, 'I know you. I know what you are, you see. I know.'

Claire got a grip on my arm and began to pull me away. 'Yes, well, that'll be all. Just tell your boy we called in, and that we'll be expecting to hear from him shortly. Just tell him that. Goodbye.'

She didn't give her white sandals a second thought as we scurried back across the field to the car. Only when we were safely shut inside and Claire had started the engine did I dare look back. The door of the caravan was shut, the old man nowhere to be seen. I leaned my head against the window, feeling the glass cool against my hot cheek, and listened to my own breathing. My breath came pantingly, shallow and fast. I couldn't bear to think of his eyes on mine . . . If Claire had not been with me, I should not have escaped. I wouldn't have been able to run.

'The smell!' said Claire. 'Made me wonder what sort of toilet facilities they have – although it was

59

more likely bad food. Certainly completely unhygienic, that wee box, no running water, no electricity. It shouldn't be allowed, not with a child living there. I'm having a word ... getting social services onto his case. There's something *seriously* wrong with that old chap.'

As the speed of the car put more and more distance between us and the caravan I began to breathe more normally, and the prickling of my skin gradually died away as the old man's evil gaze faded into memory. 'Do you think he's crazy?'

'Absolutely barking, dear girl.'

'Did you hear what he said to me?'

'Oh, I shouldn't think he was talking to *you*. I saw his eyes. Heaven knows what they were seeing, but it wasn't you. Delusions, if not the DTs. Oh, yes, I'm putting social services onto his case right away.'

A camera shop in Oban offered a film developing service in under two hours, so I left my roll of film with them before going to the swimming pool. I did my best to put the old man out of my mind, as Claire had advised, but it was impossible. Yes, sure, I'd escaped, he was no threat to me – but what about Fin? What would happen to him? I couldn't think how he could bear it, living like that, with that creature, in that rank-smelling box on the edge of the sea. No wonder he spent so much time roaming the countryside.

Over lunch with Claire, she told me more about her plans to rescue Fin.

'Don't worry, we're going to work things out for your friend,' she said firmly. 'I'm known to the head of social services for this area, and a word from me will be heard. They'll send someone out to the caravan, and one whiff of that place would convince anyone it's no place for a child.'

'Fin's not a child.'

'He's under sixteen; he certainly is. He deserves a better life, and I'm sure the council can provide it, no matter how they moan about a housing shortage.'

'What about the old man?'

'Well . . .' She chewed this one over mentally while her jaws ground away at a rare steak. 'He needs help, too, obviously. I suppose it depends a lot on how he reacts. If he's willing to be rehoused. If he'll let himself be helped. If we just happened to see him on a particularly bad day. . . . Maybe he's a drunk, maybe he could be sobered up. If not, well, Fin might be taken into care.'

My stomach clenched. I imagined some great, grey, featureless institution, boys in metal-framed beds in an echoing ward. 'Where would they send him?'

'I imagine they'd try to place him with a family in the area. Since he's already settled in at Mealdarroch Academy, they wouldn't want to disrupt his life too much. But I suppose it depends on what's available. And he might have other family somewhere else, who could take him in – what happened to his mother, do you know?'

'He said she dumped him on her sister when he

was tiny, and then later the sister got a new boy-friend who didn't like him . . .' I stopped, and she filled in the blank for herself.

'So Fin was dumped on his grandfather. Poor boy, being shuffled around like that . . . He might not be entirely happy, having to change yet again, but it's in his best interest. Maybe the old man was all right when he first took the boy in, but he's senile now, or worse. We have to get the boy away from him.' She gave me an approving smile. 'Fin doesn't know how lucky he is to have met you!'

But I had the sinking feeling that Fin wouldn't agree. No matter how horrible the old man, no matter how much better off he'd be somewhere else, I just knew he wouldn't be grateful for Claire's interference.

Claire had some other errand to run after lunch, so we arranged to meet back at the car in half an hour, and I went to the camera shop on my own. Old Mr Black had cast a pall over the day, but now I began to get excited about my pictures. I was glad to have a chance to look at them first on my own, since, even though I had every intention of showing them to Claire, I was worried in case the most important shots hadn't come out properly. A black blur on the lawn could be mistaken for Gus or Lizzie and Claire would think it was a big joke.

As soon as I'd paid for them I opened the envel-ope to have a look through the prints. I passed quickly over the landscape views I'd taken during my first week in Argyll, the pictures I'd taken of Claire and she'd taken of me at the castle and looking at the seals, and then I came across one I was sure I hadn't taken: a photograph of old Mr Black.

I nearly dropped it. Then I made myself look again, more closely. Maybe it wasn't Fin's old man. It could have been almost anyone. His features were shadowy and unclear, the picture had been taken from a distance. It couldn't be mine; I knew I hadn't taken any photo like that. It had to have been dropped into my envelope by mistake.

Before taking it back to the counter to say so, I turned to the next picture. It showed the same man, even more blurred as he turned away. The next picture was a view of the man from behind, running away. And the next. The last picture was of a mass of rhododendrons and an expanse of lawn streaked with shadows – the view from my bedroom window on the previous evening.

I knew then that there had been no mix-up with someone else's film. I had taken all the photos myself. I had looked out the window and seen a panther, but the camera told me it was really a man.

I didn't show those photos to Claire. There was no way I could have explained them, no way she would have believed me. And what would she make of the idea that Fin's old man had been prowling around Fasgadh, staring up at my window, looking for me? What did *I* make of it?

Was the man in the photo Fin's old man? Although the photos didn't get any clearer no matter how often I looked at them, when I went through them again that evening in my room I still thought my first instinct had been right.

Was the panther I'd seen running along beside the road the same one I'd seen in the garden? Unless this part of Argyll was positively teeming with black panthers it had to be the same.

Which meant it was a man who'd been running along beside the car, a man who could make himself look like a panther, and that man was Malcolm Black.

But why was he after me? What had he meant when he said 'I know what you are' – was that really his insanity talking, as Claire thought? Did he mistake me for someone else?

Or maybe it was Claire he was after – the newspaper editor whose stories were drawing too much attention to his existence. Did he want to kill her, or just make her believe?

Did Fin know? Did he even suspect? That question especially haunted me. Was he in danger? Were we all in danger?

7

The Attack

I was desperate to talk to Fin about it. I could hardly wait to see him again.

I got up early on Sunday, although early rising is not one of my strong points. I knew Claire wouldn't let me out of going to church – all my life she'd shown no interest in my spiritual education, but now I was under her roof, in her care, her role as my godmother had taken on special significance for her.

So I'd decided to see Fin before church.

Before my visit to the caravan I wouldn't have expected to find him at the dun on a Sunday morning. But now I wondered if maybe he managed to be at the dun before me every time because he spent the night there. Before I'd experienced the stink of the caravan I couldn't have imagined the smelly little chamber beneath the earth as a bedroom, but now it didn't seem so bad. Especially since he wouldn't have to share it with the old man.

'You're up bright and early,' commented Claire when I came into the kitchen. 'But those don't look like church-going clothes – did you forget it's Sunday?'

I restrained myself from remarking that her old

dressing gown looked even less like church-going clothes than my own, and said that I fancied a walk before church.

'Great! Lizzie will be pleased. Walkies, Lizzie!'

The younger of the two black dogs jumped and did her little dance. Gus gave a groan that said, Count me out, but thumped his tail so as not to offend.

I bit my lip. 'I really didn't want to take her.'

'What? Don't be silly! Why ever not?' She gave me an astonished glare, and I felt my heart begin to sink, knowing I was going to lose this argument.

I said, rather desperately, 'She scares away all the animals.'

'Nonsense!'

'She does.'

'What animals?'

'I might see an otter, but not if I have a dog with me.'

'You'll never see an otter at this time of day. It might seem early to you, but not to an otter. You'd have to get up before dawn. Now, don't be unkind – look at her, you've got her hopes up, you can't disappoint her now!'

It wasn't me who'd got her hopes up, I thought, but I couldn't say it. I couldn't win. The more I protested, the more suspicious and angry Claire would be, and I didn't need that.

'Oh, all right. I'd better take her lead, just in case we meet anyone.'

I put the lead into my rucksack along with some apples and a couple of hastily-made bacon rolls.

Surely Fin would be all right with Lizzie as long as I kept her on a lead, I thought. Lizzie was such a friendly dog; she liked everybody. Maybe she'd be able to break down his fear of dogs. But if not, I could tie her to a bush or something and we could keep the wall of the dun between the dog and ourselves.

'Don't be gone more than a couple of hours,' said Claire. 'You'll want time to wash and change before we leave for church.'

'Don't worry.'

The rainclouds of the day before had all been blown away; it was bright and sunny and felt as if it would turn really hot later on.

As soon as we were over the fence and into the woods, out of sight of the house, I fastened the lead onto Lizzie's collar. She wasn't happy about it, and neither was I, being pulled a little too rapidly up the trail by her, but I could see no alternative. I didn't know what Fin would think if he saw us coming, but he might feel safer, seeing I had her on a lead, than if she was running loose.

There was no sight of him when we emerged from the woods, both of us panting, at the top of the hill; but I thought he might be hiding. It was difficult scrambling up the last bit, still keeping a hold on the lead, but I managed. At the dun, I called out his name, and listened to the echo of my voice.

There was no reply.

'Fin! Please, I need to talk to you! I can tie the dog—' As I said this I looked around rather desperately for somewhere I could tie the lead. But, as I should have remembered, there were no trees up here, and the heather and the broom were just as impossible as the occasional snaky tendril of bramble. The stones were all either too big or too small. 'I won't let her hurt you, I promise! Please, Fin!'

Fin, if he was there, didn't show himself. Lizzie was snuffling and snorting at the ground and whining like something demented. She'd caught the scent of something, and was obviously mad keen to track it down. First she'd press her trembling body hard against my legs, and then she'd go lunging off to the end of her lead, nearly pulling me off balance a couple of times.

'Lizzie! Stop that! Heel!'

The word was not in her vocabulary, alas. After teaching her that the house was not a toilet, and that sheep were not to be worried, Claire had decided that additional training was an unnecessary luxury. But she was a good-natured dog, eager to please, naturally obedient, and when I tugged at the lead and told her to follow she abandoned the scent she found so intriguing, and went with me.

I took her back down to the path through the woods, and there I found a young tree that I could tie her to. She wasn't happy about being left like that: I tried to ignore her barking, and hoped the sound wouldn't carry down to Fasgadh. I'd brought a pen and a small pad of paper with me, to leave a note in case Fin was not to be found. But now that the moment had come to write it, I didn't know what to say. I wanted to warn him, but how? I had to be clear and I had to be quick, especially with Lizzie barking her head off. Finally I settled on:

FIN: VERY URGENT I TALK TO YOU. MUST TELL YOU ABOUT DANGER TO YOU. PLEASE (underlined three times) COME TO HOUSE OR PHONE ME TODAY (underlined three times). DANNI.

I folded the note over, wrote FIN on the outside, and then put it, held down by a rock, immediately inside the entrance to his den. Then I went running back to rescue Lizzie, who turned out to have wrapped her lead so tightly around the tree in her efforts to escape that she was in danger of strangling.

The possibility of meeting Fin somewhere else in the countryside just by chance didn't seem very great, but I remembered the way he found me the first time we'd met. Maybe, especially if Lizzie got bored with me and decided to go back home, it would happen again. Anyway, it was a good day for a walk, and I was in no hurry to get back.

I let Lizzie off her lead, and immediately I was forgiven all my sins. She licked my hand and then frisked happily beside me down the forest path. I didn't call to her or try to keep her with me in any way when she went nosing off the path, scrambling through the undergrowth on her own pursuits, but she never went far before galloping back to my side. I decided to follow the branch of the path which led around the base of the hill, behind the village of Dunmore, and eventually connected with a forestry road. I could then follow the forestry road down to the main road, and so make my way back to Fasgadh. I was so used to being guided by Fin that, without him, I wanted the assurance of a known, marked route.

Lizzie stayed with me, although often out of sight, all along the path. We'd just emerged from the mixed woodlands onto the forestry track, which skirted the edge of a vast, dark and gloomy-looking pine forest, when I heard her make a peculiar low sound, somewhere between a growl and a whine.

I turned to look at her – she was a little way behind me – and saw she was standing absolutely still, her body quivering as she sniffed the air. I felt my own body hairs prickling with unease, sensing without understanding what she'd scented.

'What is it, girl?'

The words were scarcely out of my mouth when something struck me from behind: a hard, powerful blow to my back which knocked me off my feet, onto the ground. I only just managed to fling my hands up in front of my face in time to cushion my fall. I was distantly aware of Lizzie's growls, suddenly, shockingly, close to my ear, and I caught a blurred glimpse of black fur.

There was a weight on my back, pinning me down, and then it was gone. I rolled over onto my side and pushed myself up as fast as I could.

Lizzie was making sounds that chilled my blood. Her fierce growls had become yelps of agonizing pain, and, as I pushed myself up from the road I saw two big black animals rolling together in a life-or-death struggle. One was Lizzie, a large and powerful young dog. The other – bigger, heavier, and infinitely more dangerous – was the black panther.

I screamed, and then I looked around for a heavy stick or a lump of rock, anything at all which I could use against the panther, to stop it killing Lizzie. I snatched up a branch lying beside the road, but it was rotten, no weight at all, and practically crumbled in my grasp. I threw it away and, panting, searched desperately for something else. A piece of jagged rock thrust out of the soil and I scrabbled in the dirt, breaking fingernails in the attempt, and finally managed to pull it free. It was at least as big as the panther's head, and heavy. Taking it in both hands, I staggered over to the fight.

But I was too late. Lizzie was dead, her throat torn out. The panther raised its head from the dog's dead body and stared at me with yellow eyes, through a mask of blood and matted fur.

I felt as if I was choking. I wanted to throw up, but, if I did, I was as good as dead. I knew, instinctively, that if I showed signs of weakness the beast would leap at my throat and kill me even more swiftly than it had killed Lizzie. I couldn't possibly outrun it, and I had absolutely no defence against its claws and teeth except the rock I was holding, with trembling arms, at chest-level.

If only I'd been quicker, I might have smashed its head in before it could tear Lizzie's throat out. Poor Lizzie, she'd done her best, she'd given me my best chance, losing her life in the process, and it still hadn't been enough. I didn't trust my aim enough to risk throwing away my only potential weapon, so there we were, stalemated, staring at each other, still and silent except for my own, panting breathing.

The panther stared at me for what seemed like a long time. Was it judging the odds, weighing the dangers of an attack? Or was it trying to communicate? I was afraid to move or say a word, in case, by breaking the eerie stillness which we shared, I provoked it to attack.

Then, finally, the panther turned aside. Stepping around Lizzie's body, not even giving it a glance, it left the road with one leap up the short incline into the forest.

I moved then, too, and hurled the rock after it with all my strength. But the long strain of holding it weakened my throw. The stone hit the ground short of the tree-line and rolled down the slope, where it came to rest on the road, not far from Lizzie's corpse.

8

Panther in Argyll

Kevin was in the kitchen drinking coffee with Claire when I came in. They said hello without really looking at me, and I was just taking a deep breath to break the news when Gus waddled over and nudged my hand with his moist nose.

I started crying.

'What on earth...?' Claire sounded more annoyed than worried, but Kevin got up and came over to me. 'Are you all right? Tell us what happened. Take your time. Sit down.'

I let him steer me into a kitchen chair. It was a relief not to be alone with Claire, whose responses I could never predict. He would help to calm her down, and that thought calmed me. I managed to stop crying and say, 'Lizzie's dead.'

'What!' Claire began to rise from her chair, then sat down again, clutching the edge of the table. 'What are you talking about? Where is she? What happened?'

'She was – she was trying to save me.' I bit my lip, swallowed hard, went on. 'We were on the forestry track, the one that goes up into the pine forest just after Dunmore, you know, where all those dead

73

trees are? The black panther came out of the woods—'

'Oh, honestly, you are the limit!' Claire exploded. 'Winding me up like that! Where's Lizzie?'

'She's dead. It killed her. I'm telling the truth! First, it knocked me down, then Lizzie went after it, and they fought, and it killed her. The panther ripped her throat out.'

'A panther,' said Claire scornfully.

'Yes!'

'I don't believe you.'

'I don't believe *you*! Why would I make up something like that?'

'I don't know. Why would you?' She cocked her head, giving me a fishy look. 'Maybe to cover up for something you did, something you shouldn't have done?'

'Like what? I went for a walk. I took Lizzie – you told me to take her! Something jumped out and knocked me down. It would have killed me if – if Lizzie hadn't been there. I got up and saw them fighting. It killed her. It was a panther. That's the truth!' I was practically shouting, but still heard Kevin's quiet question.

'Can you take us to the body?'

I looked at him and nodded.

Claire snorted. 'Oh, yes, another believer.'

'Danni's not a liar, a fantasist or a drunk – and neither am I,' he said. His voice was quiet yet somehow dangerous.

'I'm sorry, Danni. I didn't mean you were a liar.

Only – you might have been mistaken. You must have been.'

'Give us a loan of one of your guns,' said Kevin.

She opened her mouth to object, out of habit, then closed it, nodded. She looked as if she was swallowing something unpleasant, and then she said decidedly, 'We'll each take one, just in case. Even though I can't believe we'll need them.'

'You're probably right about that,' said Kevin. 'It's far too clever to hang about waiting for someone to come and get it.'

I thought of how the panther had run after the car in full view, and how it had come and waited on the lawn, letting me see it from the window; how, if I'd been someone with a gun instead of just a camera, it might be dead now. I almost said something, but then I realized if I mentioned photographs they'd want to see them, and there was no way I could explain the pictures I had. Claire didn't want to believe in an ordinary panther – a werepanther was completely out of the question.

Claire got two shot-guns out of the locked case in the upstairs hall where she kept them, and both she and Kevin changed their church-going shoes for wellington boots, and then we piled into Kevin's Land Rover. We quickly drove through Dunmore, past the church, and then turned up into the pine forest on the unmade road down which I'd come running only desperate minutes before.

'How far along?'

'Not far. Ten minutes walking, maybe. Just a little way past where the path comes out – you know the path that goes through the woods behind the village?'

'That one.' Kevin gestured, and I was astonished to see that we'd already come upon it. The scenery rolled past so swiftly when you were driven, and you took note of different landmarks than you did when you were on foot.

'Stop. Stop now. I'm sure I didn't go any farther. It happened around here somewhere.'

He stopped the Land Rover and we all got out. I felt my skin shrinking, pinching me: danger. The guns didn't make me feel any safer; in fact, the sight of a gun in Claire's hands made me seriously nervous. But I forced myself to concentrate and look around at the roadside instead of fearfully scanning the dark forest for a hint of watching eyes.

I hadn't mistaken the spot, but Lizzie's body was gone. The only evidence left of the death I'd seen was the bloodstained dirt of the road.

'It was there,' I said, pointing. 'There, that's the rock I threw at it. That's Lizzie's blood.'

'She's alive,' Claire cried. She stared at me in angry triumph. 'You see? She was hurt, but she managed to crawl away. Lizzie! Here, Lizzie,' she called, and whistled.

'She was dead! Her throat was ... gone. I wouldn't have left her if she'd been alive.'

'I'm not blaming you,' she said, coldly. 'Of course you were frightened. Something, probably a big dog, came leaping out of the forest and started fighting with Lizzie, and you panicked.'

Tears of frustration started to my eyes. 'I saw her die.'

'Dead bodies don't get up and walk.'

Kevin, who had been examining the roadside, now straightened up. 'Leopards are probably the only big cats that cache their kills. They'll drag them off and hide the body somewhere – usually in a tree, above the reach of scavengers – and then come back when it's safe to eat at leisure. I think that's what happened here.'

He probably expected me to be grateful for his support, but I said crossly, 'It wasn't a leopard; it was a black panther.'

'Black panthers are leopards. People used to think they were a separate species, but it's turned out that the colouring is just a genetic variation. In the right lighting you can sometimes make out the markings in the fur.'

'While you two enthusiasts talk about your obsession my dog could be dying on my doorstep. She was obviously badly injured, but I'm sure she would have made for home. Now—'

'She's dead, Claire. Lizzie's dead,' Kevin said. 'Danni saw her killed. Why won't you believe her?' He answered his own question. 'You don't *want* to believe her, that's all. This area is your shelter, your retreat, and you simply can't accept that there could be anything to disrupt the safe haven you've so carefully made for yourself. So you find some reason to disbelieve every eyewitness report, including Danni's, including mine.'

I looked at him in surprise: he'd seen the panther too!

'You'd been drinking that night—'

'Two beers. And I wasn't drinking the second time I caught sight of it, at five o'clock in the morning, then – or the third or fourth.'

'I didn't know you'd seen it four times!'

'Five, at least. Well, why should I tell you? You didn't believe me the first two times. A chap gets sensitive about being called a drunk and a dreamer, you know.'

'It's not that I think you're lying, or Danni either,' Claire said slowly. 'But eyewitness reports aren't hard evidence. People can get confused by, well, distance, or the light, or—'

'You want hard evidence? What would you make of a sheep's carcass in the branches of a tree? A full-grown sheep. There simply aren't any native predators which would not only tackle prey of that size but drag it away and cache it in a tree for later. Nothing could do that except a leopard – or a man.' He added that last with a little shrug. It made me jump and stare at him, but he didn't mean anything special by it. He was just being precise, anticipating Claire's objections.

'Well, excuse me for doubting your word, Kev, but *I* didn't see any sheep's carcass in a tree. And it could have been put there by a man. People do the strangest things, sometimes for no reason at all.'

'And you don't believe anything you don't see for yourself.'

She shrugged. 'Just a little quirk of mine.'

'Take a look at these tracks, then.'

'What tracks?'

'Over here, in the mud – the mud made partly by Lizzie's blood.'

I hurried over to look where he was pointing, and there was one, absolutely clear print by the side of the road, as well as others, more blurred, going up the embankment. But, as I expected, Claire refused to accept it for what it was.

'That's one of Lizzie's footprints.'

'No. If it was a dog there would be claw-marks. The leopard retracts its claws when it doesn't need them for fighting or climbing; a dog can't do that. Also, the shape and size are different, although I wouldn't expect you to be able to recognize that without a sample to set beside it.

'I've come across leopard prints before, out on the hills, once I started hunting for them, but not many, rarely one so unmistakable. The big cats don't often leave readable tracks because they walk so lightly, but in this case, it would have been weighed down by Lizzie's body, and it would have had to press down rather hard as it leaped up away from the road.'

Claire was staring, stony-faced, into the woods above the road. 'It could have been a dog. Danni might have been mistaken. It could have been another, bigger, black dog. Lizzie might just be hurt. She could be limping home right now.'

'And if not?' he asked.

'If something killed my dog – if it was a panther, or a leopard, or whatever it was, and it's still out there, it won't be for long. I'll find it and kill it myself.'

That evening I had two telephone calls. The first was from my mother in New York. I told her what had happened to Lizzie and, of course, she was horrified.

'Darling! How dreadful! Are you all right?'

'It didn't hurt me.' I remembered what I'd found when I'd changed my clothes (Claire having been insistent on going to church as if everything was as usual), the four, small, blood-stained rips in my T-shirt, the pin-prick markings on my back where the wickedly sharp claws had touched and then retracted instead of slashing. But they didn't hurt and I hadn't even felt the tiny cuts when they happened. It was almost, I thought, as if it had wanted to let me know that it could hurt me, but would not. 'I think Claire's more upset than I am. Well, it was her dog. And she didn't want to believe there was a panther.'

'A panther in Argyll! Who'd imagine such a thing?'

'Her newspaper's been full of stories about it, only *she* never believed any of the people who saw it.'

'No, that's typical. To hear Claire go on about it, her little pocket paradise is Eden before the Fall, without a serpent. The milk of human kindness runs through everybody's veins, there's no crime barring that committed by a few ne'er-do-wells who've all come up from Glasgow anyway, and the only people who get hurt are those who put themselves at risk by going out to sea in a storm, or up a mountain in mid-winter. Of course she wouldn't want to believe there could be a large, predatory animal roaming the hills behind her house . . . But,' she suddenly wailed, 'Oh, sweetheart, I thought I was sending you to such a safe place! I'm so sorry!'

'It's not your fault.'

'No, but, if I'd known . . . Anyway, I thought those sort of creatures only managed to survive because they never attacked human beings?'

'It didn't actually attack me – it was Lizzie. It might not even have killed her if she hadn't been trying to defend me.'

'All the same, it sounds like a very dangerous animal. Surely it will be hunted down and killed very soon.'

'I think Claire's hoping to do that.'

'She tells me she's a crack shot – but she also says she hates hunting. Which reminds me: she said something the last time I spoke to her about teaching you to shoot. Are you really interested?'

I had practically forgotten that conversation, so much had happened since, but now I thought that if I'd had a gun instead of a just a rock, Lizzie would still be alive. 'Yes! Dad thinks I should learn. I'm not sure I like the idea of shooting things just for fun, but as there's a killer out there. . . . I'd be much safer with a gun.'

I heard her catch her breath. 'Danni – you don't need a gun. Just stay out of the woods.'

'I wasn't even in the woods when it happened. I was on the road – well, a forestry road.'

'But now that you know it's not safe—'

'Nowhere is safe! I saw it – it could come into the garden if it wanted. Are you saying I should stay locked up indoors all the time because of it?'

'Not locked up . . . there must be other things to do besides wandering around the countryside by yourself. What about your friend? Fin?'

'I'm usually with him. I was only on my own this morning because Claire asked me to walk the dog. I'd be safe enough with Fin, don't you think?'

'Well . . . yes . . . oh, darling, do be careful!'

'Don't worry.'

'I can't help worrying; it's part of a mother's job-description. Oh, dear. I know you're quite sensible most of the time—'

'Thank you very much,' I said sarcastically.

'But you are so far away, and I can't help wishing . . . Oh, I do miss you, you know. I wish I could see you.'

'You will, soon. It's only a few more weeks.' I thought, as I spoke, that I sounded more like the mother talking to her child, and concentrated on that as a way of ignoring the lurch in my stomach at the thought of leaving Scotland. I didn't want to think about how much I would miss this place when I was back at home.

Sometimes I thought my mother hadn't a clue, but then at other times, when I least wanted her to, she seemed to read my mind.

'You're not sorry you went to Claire's, are you?

I mean, you are enjoying yourself? Apart from this awful business of the dog getting killed.'

'Yes.'

'You've sounded so happy, so interested in everything, and I was so glad to hear you'd made a friend . . . what I'm saying is, it's hard for me to judge from so far away, with just these phone calls – but it does seem, from what you've told me, and your dad, and what Claire has said, that you've really settled down well, that you like it there, that you feel at home.'

She was practically forcing me to think about how much I would miss, what I would be giving up, at the end of the summer. I said, 'This isn't my home.'

'But you are happy?'

'Yes.'

After we said goodbye, I went on sitting by the telephone, by myself, just thinking about the things I usually pushed out of my mind. I'd never had a friend before Fin – not ever, unless I could believe what my mother had told me about Claire when I was tiny, and counted her. I certainly didn't think of her as a friend now. She was just another grown-up who had to be tolerated and placated, like the teachers at school. Only teachers were easier, because you didn't have to live with them, and because they weren't generally so changeable and prickly as Claire. You didn't have to work at figuring out what teachers wanted. Everybody knew what was expected. You had to pay attention in class, do the work they assigned, and get things right – I didn't always manage it, but at least I knew what was wanted. With Claire, I didn't even know where to start.

I felt that way about most people, to tell the truth. I'd never understood what people did to make friends, or why nobody liked me. It wasn't that people hated me or were awful to me, just that I never had a friend. I tried, but nothing worked. I felt like a foreigner watching other girls pair off at school, as if they shared a language I couldn't understand.

Until I met Fin. With Fin, I hadn't had to try. From the very start it was as if we'd known each other a long time.

The phone rang, and I picked it up. There was Fin's voice in my ear, as if he'd felt me thinking about him.

'I found your note,' he said. 'What's wrong?'

I hardly knew where to start. So much had happened since I'd left that note. 'Your old man,' I began, and then I stopped. If he didn't know already, would he believe me?

'What about him?'

'I – I saw him.'

'How? Where? Oh – you didn't go there?' He sounded despairing.

'Yes. Oh, Fin, do you know about—' I looked around, cautiously, but there was no one to overhear. I was on the telephone in the front hall, beside the stairs, and Claire had gone back to watch her television programme in the sitting room. 'Do you know about the panther?'

'Yes.'

Did he? One cryptic monosyllable ... but then my question had been equally ambiguous. He might mean he knew about his old man, or that he'd seen the panther. I pressed on, rather than waste time. 'He attacked me today. He killed Lizzie!'

'Who? Who's Lizzie?'

'Claire's dog. The panther ripped her throat out.'

'Oh, a dog. I thought you meant he'd killed somebody. I knew he wouldn't hurt *you*.'

'He would have if Lizzie hadn't been there!'

'No.'

I shook my head in frustration. 'Look, this happened to me, not you!'

'But it happened to me first. You shouldn't have gone to the caravan, you shouldn't have let him see you.'

A shiver went down my spine. 'What do you mean? Look, we have to talk. There are so many things – it's no good over the phone. We have to meet.'

'Tomorrow, as usual.'

'Not at the dun,' I said, just as the pips went.

'Where, then?'

'Mealdarroch. The cafe.'

'Mealdarroch! Oh, come on, Danni, if you want to talk—'

'I'll be in the cafe at ten o'clock,' I said loudly, and hoped he heard me before we were cut off.

9

Fin Explains

He pushed open the heavy door of the cafe just a few minutes after ten and walked over to where I was sitting.

He looked ill at ease, fidgeting beside the table.

'Sit down, I'll buy you a bacon roll.'

'We can't talk about – the things you want to talk about – in here.'

I looked around. There were three other customers, and although the video game in the far corner made a fair amount of noise I couldn't be sure we wouldn't be overheard. So I nodded, and slid out of the booth, leaving my tea untouched. 'Want to sit on the harbour wall?'

'Could you get me that bacon roll to go, but?'

I bought two bacon rolls and a carton of juice for myself and then we strolled down to the seafront. We had it practically to ourselves, except for the seagulls. It was a still, sullen day, threatening rain. The yachts rocked and creaked gently on the water. We settled onto the seawall and didn't speak as we munched our rolls. We didn't speak, but we were getting comfortable with each other, and it was easier than I'd thought it would be when I told him about the black panther I'd seen on the lawn of Fasgadh, and showed him the photographs I'd taken.

'Was this *before* you went to the caravan?'

I nodded, although it seemed an odd first question.

'So he knew about you already. How, I wonder?'

'What do you mean, he knew about me?'

'When he . . . you said the panther attacked you. What actually happened?'

I told him about being leaped on from behind, and how Lizzie, bravely rushing to my defence, was forced into the fight which had ended with her death.

'Did he scratch you or bite you, but? Did he draw blood?'

The scratches on my back were scarcely more than pin-pricks, but now I felt them itching and burning, and I stared at him in horror, wondering what it meant and how he knew.

'Look.' He pushed up his sleeve and displayed his left upper arm. I saw two small pale marks which might have been chicken-pox scars, or the reminder of a long-ago puncture. 'That's where he bit me, to make me understand.'

'Understand what? I don't understand anything!'

'It's about the animal spirit. Not many people have it; I think it's dying out, it's really no use in the modern world. But in the olden times, and before big cities – even then, it wouldn't be in many people, but it was recognized and understood when someone was born with the animal spirit. You know the name of the dun – it was the dun of the black dog people. When someone among them was born with the animal spirit he, or she, could change into a black dog. That's what I think, anyway.'

'So you're saying your old man was born with the animal spirit, and that means he can change into a panther whenever he wants?'

'Yes. And so was I, and so were you.'

'Me!' I nearly fell off the wall. I clutched at it with both hands, feeling my heart pounding. 'No way! I've never—'

'Only because you didn't know you could.' He gazed at me quite calmly, as if what he was saying was perfectly reasonable. Although it was not a hot day, I broke into a sweat.

'I don't believe you. Why should I have this animal spirit if it's so rare – and how would *he* know, and how would you, if even I didn't know it about myself?'

'Remember the first night you were here, at the Inn, when we first saw each other?'

'How could I forget?'

'You were going on about how there couldn't possibly be a panther in Argyll—'

'Spare me, please, I remember.'

He went on, determined to make his point. 'Well, I decided to teach you a lesson. Just for a wee bit of fun, like. I thought you were a tourist I'd never meet again, and if Mrs Tinker saw me, too, well, that would be one in *her* eye, too, and serve her right for printing stories she thought were rubbish.

'So I went out of there, and I waited around till I saw your car, and then I followed you. I changed into a panther, and I ran alongside the car, and I let you have a good look at me.'

He had to be telling the truth. No one else knew about that encounter – no one but me and the panther.

'That was you? I thought, when I saw the panther in the garden, the one I took the picture of, I thought it was stalking me.'

'The old man would have seen the same thing I saw, when he looked at you. It's something you can see only through your animal eyes, that's why I didn't see it when we looked at each other in the bar.'

'See what?'

'The animal spirit. It's a kind of—' he hesitated, frowning. 'Kind of like a light, or a special colour like no other, that shines out of the eyes of someone who has it. The old man saw it in me, one night when he was passing through my town. He shouldn't have been out, not as a panther, not on that street – I never did find out what he was up to just then. Come to that, I shouldn't have been out either, but my Auntie's boyfriend had locked me out to teach me a lesson – I don't remember what for.'

'And then he – the panther – bit you?'

'No, not just then. He came back as a man, first, to tell me what I was, and to tell me what he was going to do.' Fin gave me a puzzled frown. 'That's why I don't understand ... He should have done that with you. He should have talked to you first.

Didn't he say anything? When you saw him at the caravan?'

'No. He just said – "I know you. I know what you are" – something creepy like that.'

'Maybe . . . maybe he thought that was all he had to say. Maybe he thought you understood.' Fin shook his head and worried at his lower lip with his front teeth. 'Something's happened to him. Lately, he forgets . . . Even when he looks like a man he doesn't act as he should. It's like he's forgotten how to be human. Or maybe he just doesn't care.'

I shuddered. 'Fin, you shouldn't be staying with him.'

He shrugged off my concern. 'I can take care of myself. I don't see too much of him just now, anyway.'

'He's crazy. He should be locked up.'

Fin went very still. His gaze was icy. 'You couldn't say it like that if you knew what it meant. Locked up. Not to be free. It would kill him to be locked up.'

The marks on my back itched and burned.

'What happens to me now?' I asked. 'Do I turn into a panther when the moon is full?'

'Not unless you want to.'

I gave him a sharp look. 'You mean that? If I want to? Why the scratch? Not that it was much of a scratch . . .'

He shrugged. 'I don't know. That's how it works: the human skin has to be broken to let the animal spirit out. But it's not something separate that gets out, it's a part of you, and you have to decide if you want to be your human self or your animal self just then. You make the choice, like choosing whether to walk or run.'

There had been an uneasy feeling in my stomach, and until then it had been fear. Now the feeling changed to excitement.

'So how do I do it? How do I "choose" to be a panther?'

'I can't tell you that.'

'The old man?'

Unexpectedly, he laughed. 'If you could see your face! No, you don't need him, don't worry. He didn't teach me, either. It isn't something that has to be taught – you'll find it in yourself, when the time is right.'

'Oh, honestly, what's that supposed to mean? When the time's right!' I felt cheated. 'And I guess when I can't do it you'll just say the time wasn't right . . . and it never will be. This is all some trick, isn't it? It's, I don't know, hypnotism or something. Your old man can make people think he's a panther, like a conjuring trick. He probably cut poor Lizzie's throat with a knife. Or maybe there is a real panther, and the two of you keep it hidden away in that stinky caravan when you're not sending it out to terrorize people.'

'There's no trick. It's not a trick.'

'I don't believe you. You can't turn yourself into a panther – you were lying, weren't you?'

He stared out at the harbour. 'Believe what you like.'

I felt horrible, being so nasty to him. He was my friend, after all. But if he was lying? 'If you can do it, why don't you change right now and show me?'

'Don't be daft.'

'Why not? Because other people would see?' I looked around. There were a couple of tourists taking pictures of the boats, and a little boy with his mother feeding the swans. Behind us, along Harbour Street, a man was getting money from the hole-in-the-wall bank, two women were standing in front of the village shop having a gossip, and a huddle of teenage boys were making their way towards the cafe. 'So what? They wouldn't believe their eyes. And they'd never catch you if you ran. You let *me* see you when you ran along beside Claire's car – if that really was you. So what's the difference?'

He sighed. 'It doesn't work like that. I can't just change because you ask me to. I have to want to.'

'Oh, yes, the right time, the right place. Well, I think if you can do it at all you can do it any time – here and now.'

'Oh, aye? And if I ask you to show me how you fall asleep, right here and now this minute, you can do that?'

'That's different.'

He shrugged and looked away, then looked back and met my eyes. 'This is no game, Danni. I wouldn't have told you about it at all if the old man hadn't – pushed things.'

'Why not? Why not tell me, if it's true? Why

shouldn't I know, if I have this animal spirit? Do you wish you didn't?'

'It was different for me. Nobody wanted me. I hated the way I was living. He took me away from that, gave me a whole new life. It was a way out for me. It wouldn't be the same for you.'

'Why not?'

'Once you've let it out, once you've run as a panther . . . it's not easy to give up that life. You might not be able to give it up.'

'Well, why should I? If I like it.'

'You're going back down South in – what is it, two weeks? Two weeks of freedom here, running everywhere in the hills whenever you want and then, bang, you're back in a wee house with your parents telling you when you have to come in and when you can go out. And what good would it do you to sneak out, with nothing but the city streets to run through? It's no place for an animal, the city.'

It seemed a wholly unreal argument to me, to refuse to try something new because you might not be able to do it again later, or you could but it wouldn't be the same. Either way, it seemed to me, I would lose out, so why not go for it?

'You just let me worry about that, OK? I want to try being a panther.'

'That's your choice.'

'Well?' I widened my eyes at him.

He got to his feet. 'Come on, then. First thing is to get away from all these people and buildings. I'm not making any promises. I can't *teach* you to change, but I'll try to help, the way the old man helped me. It's something inside you, remember that. It's *your* power, in your own control, and if you really want to do it, if you really want to change, you will.'

10

A Time of Changes

We walked out of Mealdarroch on the main road for about half a mile, then followed a track up the hill. The farther we went away from the town and other people the better I felt. I breathed in fresh air with its sea-tang and the smells of peppery gorse and green growing things; smells of earth and water I hadn't known before this summer, but which were now as familiar and welcome as the smell of home. I felt a part of this place. Was this feeling, I wondered, evidence that I had the animal spirit?

I wanted to believe it; I wanted the magic to happen. But I had no idea what to do.

Fin was no help.

'Tell me what to do!'

He looked exasperated. 'I can't.'

'Then tell me what *you* do.'

He went still for a moment, an inward look on his face, then he shrugged. 'It's not something I do, really ... more a way of feeling. Try ... no, don't try. Just let go: let go of your self. Forget your name, forget who you are, what other people think you are, don't worry about what anything is like – just *be*.'

He might as well have been speaking Chinese for

all the good his advice did me. I tried to imagine myself into a panther's skin. When I was tiny I loved playing at being an animal, and I could remember the way the world had changed then, the way our small garden became a big, grassy meadow, and how sweet the grass had tasted to my horse-self.

But I wasn't an infant now, and I didn't want to play pretend. I wanted it to be real; I wanted to discover my own special powers, not just imagine that I had them. But maybe it was like trying to fall asleep: the more I thought about it, worried about it, and pursued it, the more it eluded me.

After some time of struggling to concentrate on not being who I thought I was, closing my eyes and then opening them in the hopes of surprising a panther's-eye view of the world, I began to doubt. How could it be that I'd had this power inside me since I was born, yet had never known it? Would I have gone on until I died without knowing if I'd never met Fin?

I didn't like doubting my friend, but what if he wasn't really my friend? What if he'd been leading me on, setting me up, and was now laughing at me behind that solemn face?

Finally, we quarrelled. I asked him to prove that what he'd said was true. If he couldn't turn me into a panther, fair enough, but he could at least let me watch him change himself. He wouldn't do it, and it turned into a showdown, both of us getting more and more furiously stubborn until finally I stalked off and walked back to Mealdarroch by myself.

After I'd cooled down, I was sorry. I missed Fin, and I knew it was my own fault that I'd lost the only friend I'd ever had. Without him, the days were long and dull. I wasn't allowed to go out roaming the hills on my own since Lizzie had been killed – not that I wanted to, anyway – and rather than spend the whole day cooped up in the house, I generally went into Mealdarroch with Claire.

She didn't have the sort of job that kept her in the office all day, and apart from printing deadlines and the occasional crisis, she could pretty much set her own hours. She took me along with her on interviews, and to view the prize-winning livestock at a local fair, and she also took time off to take me to places she thought I'd enjoy. Claire was very good to me, and I tried to be grateful, but I kept feeling that we were both just pretending to be friends, which made me miss Fin more than ever.

Always at the back of my mind was the thought that nothing that happened now really mattered, because this time would soon be history, and I'd be home. It wasn't so much that I was looking forward to anything at home – in fact, I dreaded September when I'd have to go back to school – but at least it was where I belonged, and no matter how dull my life there, it was at least ordinary and under-standable.

I had just started on the final countdown – ten days to go – when Mum telephoned from New York to tell me she'd been offered a six-month contract.

'Where?'

'Here, in New York. But it's only six months—'

'You didn't say yes?'

'Danni, this is the best opportunity of my entire career! I couldn't say no.'

'You're going to stay in New York for another six months?'

'I know it sounds a long time, darling, but it will fly, really it will. You'll be so busy with school and things, and the money's very good. You could come over here for your school holidays; how do you fancy Christmas in New York?'

'What does Dad say?'

There was a pause. It wasn't very long, but in it I could hear the vast distance between us. She said, very carefully, 'Your dad and I have decided ... well, we've agreed that some time apart would be a good thing at the moment, so that we can think about our relationship.'

I felt sick. 'What does that mean, think about your relationship? Why can't you think about it together? You're married!'

'Don't get upset. It's only a little time apart, so we can think about what we both want, and what's for the best, without arguing about it.'

I felt doubly betrayed. I'd talked with Dad only the night before, and he hadn't so much as hinted that he wasn't looking forward to my mother's return or that anything was wrong. I wanted to shout that she and my dad weren't allowed to separate, that they must not even think about divorce – but she hadn't said that word, and I didn't want to be the first, so I didn't say anything.

'Danni, are you there? Sweetheart, try to think of this as a challenge. You're a big girl now, and you can use this as an opportunity to become more independent, as well as to make new friends and learn new skills. We've both been so pleased that you like Scotland so much. I always knew you'd get on with Claire, of course. I feel so much better about staying knowing that you're happy, too.'

I couldn't believe what she was saying. 'But I'm going home next week.'

'No, darling. Your father and I – and Claire, of course – have decided that it would be best for you to stay in Scotland while I'm over here.'

'When did you decide this?' I demanded. 'You said when I came that it was for five weeks – now it's six months – next thing, it'll be seven years! Why don't you admit it – you've dumped me on Claire for ever, and you're never coming back!'

'Danni, calm down, please. It's not for ever, and I've given it a lot of thought.'

'Oh, yeah? What about school?'

'You'll go to the local school. It has a very good reputation.'

'It's not fair, it's just not fair!' I wailed. 'I can't believe this! You decide you want a new life, so Dad and I get dumped like old clothes that don't fit you any more!'

'It's not like that. I know it might seem rather sudden—'

'It doesn't just *seem* sudden—'

'Look, I wasn't expecting this job offer—'

'You didn't have to take it.'

'But when it came, it just made so much sense. For both of us. You were sounding so happy at Claire's—'

'For a holiday, yeah, but that doesn't mean I want to live here!'

'—and she loves having you, she really does. And then there's school. Please don't tell me you'll miss your old school! We would have sent you somewhere else, this year or next, if only we could work out the finances – well, we don't have to take out a second mortgage to get you into Mealdarroch Academy.'

'So I stay here for the next four or five years, is that what you're saying? Without discussing it with me, without even seeing the school, you just decide that this is where I'm going to live, without you, until I'm old enough to leave school?' My voice was very flat; even as I said the words, I couldn't believe she meant it. It was as if I'd been orphaned – but my parents were still alive.

'No, of course not. Darling – just give it one term, all right? It gets you out of that dreadful school at home, and gives us all some breathing space while we plan the next move. There are so many things to think about and discuss – I know it's all rather sudden, but sometimes things happen, and you have to make decisions rather quickly. It can't be a bad thing to get you away from that dreadful school. It's not as if you were happy there, or had friends – and you've already made one new friend where you are.'

'We've fallen out,' I said bitterly.

'Oh, Danni. Don't struggle so. I want you to be happy – so does your father. Why can't you let yourself be happy? Give it a chance. Try the new school just until Christmas. Then we'll be together – I'll fly home, or you can come over here, your choice – and we can talk about it and decide what's best.'

'We don't have to wait until Christmas. I already know what's best for me – and for you and Dad. We should be living together, in our own home, like always. It doesn't matter what school I go to. If this job of yours is really so wonderful and important, then Dad should give up his, and we can all go live in New York.'

'Danni, I'm sorry, but that is not possible.' I hadn't heard that tone of voice very often, but I recognized it as the one that would not be argued with, steely and deaf. 'You'll stay with Claire, and go to Mealdarroch Academy—'

'No!' I shouted. 'I will not stay with Claire! You can't make me! You don't run my life any more – you don't have that right. You want to live by yourself, OK, but you can't tell me and Dad what to do – I'm staying with him!'

I slammed down the receiver – the first time in my life I'd ever hung up on anyone – and immediately jabbed in the digits of my home number.

The answering machine picked up. It was well past the time Dad usually got home from work, so I hoped he was listening.

'Dad,' I said after the beep. 'Are you there? Please pick the phone up! It's Danni, and I need to talk to

101

you. Please, Dad.' I bit my lip. Maybe he was in the garden, or had gone out for a takeaway? 'Please call me right away, as soon as you get in, no matter what time it is. I'm desperate.'

With a sinking heart, I hung up. It would have been better not to leave a message, I thought. Even as I was talking I'd realized that he would be behind this change in my life as firmly as my mother. Even if this separation was my mother's idea, even if he wanted her to come home, they would have agreed on what was best for me. He and Mum might argue about some things, but they both agreed my school was a disgrace. Suddenly the conversations we'd had recently, about boarding school, made a new and sinister kind of sense. I'd thought he was only imagining what we might do if Mum began making more money; now I realized he'd been sounding me out about living away from home, trying to prepare me for what he already knew was going to happen in a too-subtle way. I wasn't going to be allowed to go home; I didn't have a home any more. Unless I became a genius overnight and won a scholarship somewhere else, Mealdarroch Academy was my future.

My stomach twisted as I remembered saying to Fin, 'People can't just throw their kids out like that!' How innocent I'd been; how smug and stupid. I didn't fit in with my parents' new life-styles, so they'd dumped me.

Just then, Claire opened the sitting-room door and came creeping out, smiling falsely. 'Good news, I hope?'

I snarled, and she rearranged her expression. 'Oh, dear. I was hoping you'd be pleased. From what you'd told me about your school, I thought you'd be wanting a change. And Mealdarroch Academy is very highly regarded.'

I was sick of hearing about what a great school it was. 'There's more to life than going to school.'

'Well, of course there is. But I thought you were happy here. I've certainly enjoyed your company. And I thought, especially in the last week, that we were getting along so well. Is the idea of spending six months at Fasgadh really so dreadful?'

'I'm not staying,' I said shortly. 'I'm going back to live with my Dad. That's where my home is, whatever Mum decides to do.'

'Now, Danni. Your father—'

'He said I could. Just now.' I gestured at the telephone.

'I doubt that very much.'

'Doubt all you like, that's what he said.' I glared at her. 'He doesn't think I'm safe here. I told him what happened to Lizzie, and he said I must come home at once.'

She sighed, looking as long-suffering as if she'd been putting up with my pathetic lies for years. 'I've spoken to both your parents, and we've all agreed—'

'Well, that's fine for you, only I didn't agree to anything!'

'There's no need to shout.'

'Oh, yes there is!' And, shutting my eyes, I opened my mouth and screamed at the top of my lungs for as long as I could manage. When I finished I felt weak and wobbly, but also strangely energized. Claire had left me to it. Before she could come back I made my escape out the front door and ran around the house, through the back garden, over the fence and into the woods.

I didn't think about where I was going. I was driven by rage and the overwhelming urge to escape. I gave no thought to the fact that it was nearly dark, and I scarcely noticed when I began to run on four legs instead of two.

The change was that easy, and that swift. One moment I was a girl, helpless, frightened, powerless to get out of the trap the grown-ups had put me in – the next, I was a wild animal running free, without a care. I could see in the dark and I wasn't afraid of anything.

It was as if I'd always been what I was now. Somewhere deep inside was the memory of the girl I had been, but she stayed well back. There was no room in my cat's head for her way of thinking and being, for her surprise, her fears, her caution – those things would only get in the way of my ability to function as I must. So, although I knew that 'she' was me as well, and that I might need to call on her suddenly, to let her take over again, just now, animal, I was in my element. She was pushed back into some dark corner and there, probably, went to sleep.

I couldn't waste any of my energies on her distant concerns when the world bristled, as it did, with possibilities of injury, capture and death, but also with the excitement of the hunt, the gratification of the kill and the feasting that would follow. I was cautious, but not afraid. There was no fear in me at all. I was at home in the woods, in the wilderness, in my long, fast, powerful body.

A low, challenging cry made me stop. My ears flattened against my head, and the fur came up on my back as I listened to the territorial warning of another great cat, demanding to know who I was and by what right I travelled these claimed lands.

Slowly I turned my head in the direction of the sound, and I saw two eyes glowing out of the shadowy woods. It was nearly invisible except for the eyes, and I couldn't catch its scent. I let my ears come up and altered my posture so as not to look aggressive, without actually letting down my defences or becoming submissive, and then I called out softly, identifying myself.

The other spoke again and came forward, revealing himself. Another panther, a male, a little larger but not much older than I was. His ears pointed forward and his tail was held high in greeting. And suddenly I knew him: Fin.

I stepped forward to meet him and as soon as we were close enough we gently butted heads and rubbed our faces together, inhaling deeply, exchanging greetings and welcome as we exchanged our scents.

After a moment he began to purr, and moved to stand so that the length of his body was against mine and I could feel his purr, a rumble so low that it scarcely existed as a sound outside his body. It seemed to pass from his body into mine and become a part of me, and I began to make the same sound.

In this way, we expressed our pleasure at being together, and he let me know that his territory could be mine, as well. He had shared his knowledge of the land with me when we were both human, and now, as a cat, he would do the same.

He turned away and I followed him into the wild and luminous night.

The land was alive to me in a way I could never have imagined. It hummed and flickered with life even where it seemed empty. My keen nocturnal vision was so responsive to motion that I saw it like flashes of brilliant colour against the monochrome setting of trees, rocks and plants. Sometimes the wind might fool my sight by waving the grass or a bush, but then I relied on my senses of smell to tell me whether or not to take any notice. In addition to smell, I had another sense which, as a human, I had no name for and could not have imagined: it was somewhere between smell and taste and yet it was also like the sense of touch – if you could imagine touching something as intangible as an odour.

The site of this ability seemed to be somewhere in the roof of my mouth, and extended out through my whiskers as well. With them I received messages from the air and the earth and everything around me.

Fin's name, his special scent, was written everywhere, telling me again and again that this was his territory.

Occasionally I paused to rub the side of my face against a rock or a tree to add my own signature, although I still felt uncertain about my right to do so. But Fin, when he noticed, watched tolerantly.

Then, from behind one concealing rock, something sprang out and began to run: a hare.

Fin was after it like a shot, a sleek, lethal black bullet. When he caught it, the hare screamed like a baby, and then, neck broken by the powerful crunch of the panther's jaws, it was dead.

Now that it was too late, I felt my muscles tense with the urge to give chase. Fin tossed the dead animal at my feet in a way that was both affectionate and scolding, as if he'd been my mother saying, 'There, that's how you do it!' and shaking her head at my lack of attention.

Although I seemed to have been a panther for ever, for all my life, it was not, after all, a very long life. It may seem instinctive, but cats have to learn to hunt. In a way I was like a just-weaned cub: I needed to eat, I wanted to hunt, but I still needed to learn how. I had the instincts, but not the skill. Most of all, I needed practice.

The smell of fresh meat brought saliva pooling in my mouth but I didn't dare touch it. I hadn't killed it myself, and punishment for taking someone else's food might be severe.

Fin gave a brief, low rumble. He put his head down to sniff the body of the animal he'd just killed and then, catching it in his mouth, he tore it apart and tossed one piece to me. At the first hot, sweet taste of blood I couldn't resist. The bones crunched

107

tenderly between my jaws and the thick, chewy meat almost dissolved on my tongue.

Half a hare was only a morsel to the beast I'd become. It was gone too soon, leaving my appetite whetted, making me hungry for more.

I knew that Fin felt the same. Now as we moved through the countryside it was with a single, sharp purpose. No more leisurely marking or checking of boundaries – we were on the prowl for prey.

But, as if the cry of the slaughtered hare had been a warning, nothing now stirred. All the other hares had run and the rabbits were in their burrows, safely hidden in their dreams; the birds were quiet on their nests. Now and then I would pick up a whiff of deer, and eventually we caught sight of a herd picking their way across open heathland. But the wind was against us, it seemed, and the deer picked up our scent – or something else frightened them – and they bolted, in a group, long before we could get close enough for a kill.

Hunting made us hungrier, but all through the night as we travelled we had no luck. Eventually we came in view of the dun, and I realized we had been moving in a large circle. I followed Fin up to the side of the dun, and into his den beneath the outer wall. My nose twitched. I could smell Fin, but also there were human smells, and even in the darkness I could pick out the scattering of dead matches and cigarette ends lying amid the dead leaves and moss on the damp ground.

But even though humans did occasionally visit the dun – humans besides Fin and myself, I mean

– I knew that no one would disturb us here in the night. Even in daylight, should we sleep so long, there would be plenty of warning if anyone approached, time enough to escape. Humans never went anywhere quietly.

Following Fin's lead I stretched out on my side beside him. Comforted by the warmth of his body so close to my own I drifted into a light doze.

I woke abruptly. As soon as I lifted my head, Fin woke, too, and his yellow eyes met mine. I froze in terror. A panther, as near to me as the one which had killed Lizzie. The stink of it was everywhere in that small space, filling my nostrils.

In desperate panic I leaped up, and found myself on four feet, not two. I gave a cry of fright and heard, not a human voice, but a cat's pathetic moan. I tried to run but could only circle the enclosed space, unable to find my way out, driven by a terrifying sense of entrapment which had little to do with the underground chamber, everything to do with the animal body I found myself in. I ran so fast I was spinning, out of control.

A blow to my head knocked me out of orbit, back on my haunches, half-stunned. The other panther glared at me, and I understood that its paw had landed the blow that had nearly stunned me. Now, I thought, it will kill me.

'Danni,' said Fin in a low, urgent voice. 'Danni, snap out of it!' He was a boy now, no longer a panther, and he reached out to touch me, fearless, and gripped my forepaw tightly in his hand.

And all at once it wasn't a black, furry forepaw,

but a girl's tanned and dirty bare arm. I could see, not with the cat's superior night-vision, but because light sifted down to us through the stones on top and filtered into the passageway. The stink of panther still surrounded me.

I scrambled away from Fin and the den and struggled back through the narrow passageway, out into the open air.

It was light; it was morning.

With a dizzying shock, I realized I had been out all night.

Claire was going to *kill* me, I thought in despair, and I began to run. After a night on four legs I was newly clumsy on two, and I fell twice as I stumbled down the hill and made my way along the forest path back to Fasgadh.

11

What am I?

Claire must have been watching for me from the window. She opened the door from the inside just as I reached for it from the outside. We stared at each other. She looked pale and pinched. Her hand came up as if she would hit me, and then fell back to her side.

'Just where have you been?'

I couldn't tell her the truth, but a convincing lie seemed equally beyond my reach. I didn't have any friends I could pretend I'd stayed with – there was only Fin, and to say I'd spent the night in his caravan, with or without the old man, would be even worse than saying I'd slept in the woods.

'Danielle, I asked you a question. I've been up all night waiting for you. I even phoned the police. Now where have you been all this time?'

'I was out. Are you going to let me in, or not?'

Her lips narrowed still more, and then she stepped back, allowing me in. Her nose wrinkled as I passed her. 'Phew – you stink!'

'Yes, well, thanks a lot. I think I fell in something. Mind if I go up and take a bath?'

'Not until you tell me where you went when you ran out of here like that. What was on your mind?'

'Nothing! I just wanted to get out, get away and think things over, and . . . so I did. I didn't mean to stay out all night.'

'But where were you?'

'The dun—' as I began to tell the truth, I realized it might be dangerous. What if she forbade me to go there again? I stumbled and recovered as best I could with 'Dunmore.'

'Dunmore? There's nothing in Dunmore.'

'There's the church.'

'You're telling me you went to church?'

'I just wanted somewhere I could be alone, somewhere to be quiet and think.'

'I thought the church was locked at night.'

I shrugged. 'I fell asleep. The next thing I knew, it was light, so I came home.'

She stared at me and shook her head and sighed. She didn't look so angry any more, and I relaxed a little, realizing she believed my story.

'I'm thirsty. Could I have some water, please?'

'Help yourself.'

As I went towards the sink I heard a low growl. I looked around, and there was Gus in his usual spot beside the Aga, but not lying in his usual relaxed slump. His head was up, and he looked more alert than I had ever seen him. He was looking straight at me, and quivering, and growling.

I felt my muscles tense, as if in preparation for a great leap, and I showed him my teeth.

Luckily Claire was looking at Gus rather than at me. She frowned and prodded him with her foot.

'What's wrong with you, you silly dog? That's Danni! You're not to growl at Danni!'

His growl became throatier, more menacing. I went absolutely still.

'Gus!' Claire spoke sharply, as if trying to rouse him from a dream, and when that didn't work, she bent down and caught hold of his collar. He lurched to his feet, pulling away from her, towards me. 'Stop that! Right, you're going out to your kennel, since you won't be nice.'

While she was taking the dog outside, I made my escape up the stairs and into the bathroom. I knew why Gus had growled, what he had smelled, because I could still smell it on myself – the stink of the great cat. The only thing I didn't know was if I'd be able to wash it off.

I was horrified when I saw myself in the big bathroom mirror; Claire must have had her contact lenses out, I thought. If she'd realized how filthy I was she would never have believed my story of a night spent quietly inside a church. There were dead leaves caught in my hair, and my clothes, shoes and fingernails were thick with mud, as if I'd been rolling in it, as if I'd spent the whole night running and rolling and crawling around in the forests and on the hillsides.

I stared at my own very familiar girl-face in the mirror and tried to imagine my ordinary grey eyes glowing golden, with a cat's slitted pupils, or sleek black fur sprouting everywhere from the pale, faintly freckled skin and my head changing its shape in the weird, painful-looking way such transform-

113

ations happened in the movies – I remembered how the boys were turned into mice in the film of *The Witches*.

But it hadn't been like that for me – not only was it not painful, but it hadn't been gradual. It had been so quick I wasn't even aware of exchanging one form for another.

There was a crusted, brownish smear next to my mouth. As I reached up to scrape at it, I realized it was blood, and I froze, staring at it, at myself in the mirror, in absolute horror as the memory rushed through me, too vivid to be denied, of eating, raw, half a freshly-killed hare. And wanting more.

Saliva rushed thickly to my mouth, and I gagged, nearly vomiting, tasting again the metallic tang of blood in my mouth and the warm, slippery tangle of meat and tendon beneath the fur . . .

A knock at the door interrupted the nightmare. Self-preservation made me speak sharply. 'What is it?'

'Danni? I haven't finished talking to you.'

'Can't I have my bath first?'

'I just want a word.'

'Go on, then.'

'Well, open the door! I want to see you when I talk to you.'

'Just a minute, then.' I scrubbed at my face with a flannel, and then opened the door to Claire.

She was looking very serious. 'I've called the police, told them it was a false alarm. I don't want to have to do that again, Danni. There's to be no more of that, understand? No more temper tan-trums, no more staying out all night, or else.'

I stared at her. 'Or else, what? You'll send me back home? Well, hooray for that; I'll go now.'

'I thought you might have something like that in mind, so I want to tell you now, before you get too enamoured of the idea, that it won't work. I don't care what you do, your mother's not coming back until she's ready. I won't let her. She deserves a chance, and if you won't give it to her, I will.'

My jaw dropped. 'I want her to have a chance, too – more than anyone! I'm not trying to get her to come home—'

'Good.'

'I just don't see why I have to stay here with you.'

She flinched a little at that. 'Believe it or not, I actually thought you liked it here.'

'Yes, all right, it was fine for a holiday, but nobody said anything about staying on. Why can't I go home when summer's over? Why can't I go back and stay with Dad?'

'Because your Dad doesn't want you.'

It was my turn to flinch. Claire immediately looked sorry, and tried to touch me, but I moved back out of reach. 'I shouldn't have said that – of course he wants you; it's only that he doesn't want the sole responsibility while your mother's away, especially since . . . well, he told me there was some trouble. That you'd been skipping school.'

I scowled. 'I didn't get in any trouble! Well, except for skipping school. But I was in the library.

I needed more time for my homework. And it was only a few times.' Only a few times that I had been caught, anyway, I thought, but did not say.

'Your dad said if he had to go to that school, he'd skive off, too. All the same . . . you can see it must be a worry for him. And if you're not willing to go to that school, why not give Mealdarroch Academy a chance? And me?'

'Looks like I'll have to,' I said. Then, because it had sounded so grudging, added, 'I'm sorry. It's not your fault. And I really do like it here, in a lot of ways. But I liked living at home, with my Mum and Dad, the two of them together – I just don't see why that had to change.'

'Things do change, whether we want them to or not. Then we have to make the best of it. And sometimes what comes out of the change is even better than you could have hoped, before.' She looked at me appealingly. 'Danni, you may feel that you've been dumped here, but I don't. I wanted you to come, and I really am glad that you're staying. I find it hard to make friends, so when I do have a good friend, like Kevin or your mother, they're very important to me. But it's not just for your mother's sake that I've liked having you here. Since the first moment I saw you, a few hours after you were born, I've felt a connection . . . Maybe you don't feel it. But I think we are alike in some ways.'

I didn't want to hear it. I'd had that pathetic fantasy once, too, but now I knew better. I yawned. 'Sorry,' I said. 'And I'm really, really sorry about last night. I didn't do it to worry you, and I honestly didn't mean to stay out all night.'

'That's all right, then. We won't say any more about it. Now, how about a hug to say we're friends?'

I shrank away. 'I'm all dirty and smelly.'

'I'll let you have your bath. And then . . . why don't you just go on back to bed for a little while? That's what I'm going to do.'

'Yeah, I think I will.'

Still she didn't leave me, and I could feel that there was something more she wanted to say, or to ask me. Before she could work out whatever it was, I said, 'Don't worry; it won't happen again.'

But I knew, even as I spoke, that I was lying.

12
Instinct

That one night changed me for ever. There was no going back. Now I knew what I was – or at least, what I could be.

As a panther, I'd still been *me* – but I wasn't human. The 'me' that was a girl didn't exactly go away, it was still inside the animal, but as if asleep. It was the same when I was back in my human body: the panther-me was still there too. And you know how cats sleep: ready to spring into action at the first sign of trouble.

Now I thought I understood why Fin hadn't rushed to tell me about the animal spirit. Yes, it was a gift, to be able to change form, but it was a gift with a dark side. And once you'd taken it, you couldn't give it back.

I wasn't sorry for the experience. 'Enjoyed' is too weak, too narrow, too human a word for what I'd felt during my night as a panther. But afterwards I felt frightened. I didn't know if I wanted it to happen again, and I didn't know if I had any choice.

I felt desperate to talk to Fin, but it wasn't so easy.

Although she'd seemed to accept my apologies, Claire was watching me in a way she never had before. I was reminded of the way she'd once, on Kevin's boat, clung grimly to my arm, determined to stop me from jumping into the water. I'd had no intention, then, of trying to join the seals, but now there was something in the wild which called me, and somehow Claire suspected, and seemed determined to keep me from it.

When I said I wanted to stay at home, that I was too tired to go out, I knew it was no coincidence that she announced she would work from home that day. When I said I needed some air, she came out with me, and then we strolled around the garden and talked about the weather and the plants like people in a play. I wondered if Fin was hidden in the woods, watching us, and I wished like anything that we'd worked out a system of coded signals.

On Saturday, she whisked me off to Glasgow to buy the clothes and other things I'd be needing for school.

'Can't it wait?' I pleaded.

'Till when? Term starts on Tuesday.'

I stared at her in disbelieving horror. 'Next week? That can't be right! It's only the middle of August!'

'Yes, the terms are slightly different up here to down south, I believe, but it all adds up to the same number of weeks.'

'Not for me, it doesn't!' I couldn't believe it. Not only forced to go to a strange new school, but done out of two weeks of my hard-earned holidays as well.

Glasgow was a nightmare. Crowded city streets and shopping precincts had never been my favourite places, but I found them particularly hard to take just then. Claire's short-tempered nervousness didn't help, and neither did the feeling of having a restless, caged beast inside me just looking for an excuse to break free.

I made snap decisions about clothes, not caring that I'd regret my choices later. I just wanted to get it over with, to get away from the bad smells and rushing traffic, the noise and crush of human bodies.

Oh, the relief when we'd finally left the last of the city behind us, and the hills, green and brown and purple against the hazy, distant sky, came into view, looming over the cool waters of Loch Lomond. I felt as happy as at the sight of my own mother's face. I was on my way home.

I think that was the moment when I knew how much I'd changed, and stopped fighting it.

That night I went back to the dun.

I had tea with Claire, who was going out to a sort of concert called a *ceilidh* afterwards. She tried to talk me into coming along, but I pretended I'd been too wrecked by the Glasgow experience to consider anything but an early bed.

'Come on, the music will perk you up! Believe me, I know how you feel, and there's nothing like a bit of singing and dancing to make it better.'

'No, honestly, I couldn't.'

'Oh, all right, then, you young fogey! Early to bed with you, and I'll see you in the morning.'

After she'd gone, I stuffed the spare pillow and a rolled-up blanket under the duvet to mimic my sleeping body. My teddy bear had fur only a shade duller than my hair, so I positioned him at the top, just sticking out. It wouldn't fool anybody who took a close look, but if Claire took it into her head to peek in at me before she went to bed, I thought it should satisfy a casual glance.

Then I tucked my house-key deep into the small, inner pocket of my jeans, wondering as I did where it would go when there was no longer a pocket to contain it. Come to that, where did my clothes go when I changed form? I brooded on this as I left the house and as I started along the path through the woods I was just beginning to get entangled in this deeply practical question when something made me turn it over and look at it from the other side: where, when I was a girl, did my long tail lurk?

I thought of how dirty my clothes had been when I'd come back from my first night out; they'd certainly seemed to share all my experiences. Perhaps they'd turned into the panther's fur. That could make sense, I thought, walking the forest trail more by instinct than by sight in the gathering gloom: clothes were to a human being what fur was to an animal.

And then into my mind came the memory of the panther I'd seen outside my window, the photograph I had taken, the photograph which had turned out to be of the old man, and I was gripped by a dreadful thought.

What if I hadn't changed at all, not really, not physically? What if the panther form was only some sort of trick, an illusion like hypnosis? When I'd looked out my window I'd seen a black panther because the old man could somehow convince me I had. But the camera could not be hypnotized; the camera could only take a picture of what was really there. What if I'd been hypnotized – by Fin, or the old man, or even my own powerful need – into believing that I'd changed, when really I'd only believed I was an animal, running around and growling and ripping with my own human teeth at the poor little hare Fin had killed . . .

'Are you going to stand there all night for midgie meat?'

I jumped at Fin's voice. At first, in the darkness of the forest, I couldn't see him at all, but then he moved and I could.

'What's wrong?' he asked.

'How could a person turn into a panther?' I asked.

'Don't you know?'

'No. No I don't. Fin, it's not possible!'

He sighed. 'It happened.'

'Did it? Did I really turn into a panther, or did I just *think* I did?'

'What are you blethering about?'

Something in his ordinary presence, his exasperation, worked on me, and my fears became insubstantial and fluttered out of my grasp. What was I worrying about? But still I said stubbornly, 'I want to know what's real!'

He snorted. 'Oh, aye, and will you be a philosopher, or a physicist when you grow up? Don't you know you're only a mass of vibrating particles like everything else in this world? Now, will you come with me, or no?'

We stared at each other in the dim forest light. Then he shook his head, and I thought of an animal shaking off flies. 'Suit yourself,' he shrugged, and turned and walked away.

I was looking at the pale shape that was Fin's back when it disappeared. A shiver went through me. I was watching a huge black cat moving away. No hocus-pocus, no agonizing, time-consuming change, but *real magic*.

How could I have doubted it?

Especially when I could do it too?

For a split second I was held in place by a stubborn, desperately rational human mind, and then I stopped trying so hard. I didn't have to do anything, only to be, to be what I wanted. I knew what I wanted. I stopped trying so hard to be human, and went loping after the other panther on all four strong legs.

Fin had compared changing form to falling asleep, but really it was more like waking up, moving out of the confused, still nothing of sleep into the living day.

I was part of the world, connected to everything around me, a piece of the larger pattern, as I had never been (or at least, had never felt myself to be) as Danni.

We prowled our territory together, companionable, moving along pathways invisible to human eyes which took advantage of whatever cover the changeable landscape could offer: from forest to moorland, across the hillsides, from brush to rock to tree, moving swiftly as shadows across open ground and then again more slowly in more sheltered areas, in a pattern like a complex dance. My senses were always alert for prey or for danger.

Then I glimpsed movement and froze. It was the movement of something large. Although he had not seen it himself, Fin responded to my cue, becoming as motionless as one of the rocks on the hillside.

Something moved slowly across the boggy, open ground ahead of us, pausing now and then to lower its huge head and graze. It was a stag, crowned with a fine rack of horns.

For a moment the stag paused, raised his head and stared directly at us. I could see the faint quiver of his moist nose. But I knew he could not see us in the darkness, and the wind was coming from the wrong direction, and would not carry our scent. The stag didn't even suspect it was being stalked; it was cautious only out of instinct. When he turned and walked away from us, we followed.

Always we had moved lightly, carefully, but now, with our prey in view, we ran in short bursts, low to the ground, practically invisible. Whenever the stag stopped, raising its head high in meaningless challenge, to sniff the wind, we also stopped, becoming, to its weak eyes, nothing more than harmless shadows in the night. A look and a sniff and a listen, and then, falsely reassured, the big animal moved slowly on.

We came closer after every pause. Finally we had to break cover: we were in the open, with no bushes, rocks or trees between us and our prey. Fin and I both judged the moment so precisely that it was like telepathy: we had no need to exchange a look or a sound before splitting up and rushing the stag, one on each side.

The stag let out a great, bellowing cry and tried to lower his head, to use his only weapon, the great horns, against me, but I was already mid-leap before it reacted, and my teeth were sinking into its throat even as Fin, pouncing from the other side, landed straddling the stag's back, his great claws raking open the flesh of our victim's side, letting the blood flow.

It bellowed again, and then began to strangle, to drown in its own blood. The battle for this stag was lost before he knew it was begun. Beneath our combined assault, with Fin's powerful incisors scissoring away at the stag's spinal cord to paralyse him, and my own teeth ripping his throat open, the beast hadn't a chance. It fell beneath us, writhing and kicking more and more feebly, until it was dead.

The hot, sweet, salty blood filling my mouth energized me and made me wild for more. I could hear Fin growling softly as he began to feed, and, probably, I was making the same noise as I tore great chunks of warm flesh away from the carcass to satisfy my hunger.

We ate and ate until our bellies distended and we were reeling. Humans don't know what eating is all about.

Later, sated and groggy with meat, unable to swallow another scrap, we staggered away from the remains of our kill, and made our way slowly back to the dun. There, in our earth, we lay down side by side and started on the long, slow, pleasurable process of grooming ourselves, cleaning the blood and gore from our fur with long, thorough swipes of raspy tongues until the swipes became slower and finally I fell into a gentle, contented, full-stomached doze.

When I awoke to a glimpse of the lightened sky, this time I didn't panic. I gave Fin a friendly nudge with my head to tell him I was going, and then I emerged into the pre-dawn mist, and trotted away briskly down the hill and through the forest. Not until I came within sight of Claire's house did I turn back into a girl again.

And then I regretted it. Everything was suddenly darker, dimmer and strangely dead. I couldn't sense the life all around me, or feel my own natural sense of belonging. Instead, I was all too aware that I *didn't* belong, I wasn't supposed to be out here in the woods – Claire would have a fit if she knew I wasn't asleep in my bed.

I felt a powerful urge to turn around and run back to Fin. Human life was too complicated. But, with an effort, I controlled myself. It wouldn't solve anything, only make more trouble for myself, if I vanished again. Besides, I didn't know what time it was, but it must be awfully early. Claire would be in her bed, never dreaming I was not in mine. With any luck I could do just as I'd planned last night, and sneak back inside and upstairs for a few hours' kip, and no harm done, my secret safe.

I checked the house-key was still in my pocket, and then I clambered over the fence into the back garden, aware the whole time of how feeble and clumsy this little body was. It would never outrun a deer, let alone tackle one and bring it to the ground.

I'd just locked the front door behind me when my skin began to prickle with warning, and then, as I turned around to look, I heard the growl.

Gus stood at the bottom of the stairs, stiff-legged and defensive, barring my way. He showed his teeth and growled again.

I didn't plan what I did next. There was no time for thought, only for instinct. Despite what Claire said about his gentle nature, the elderly black Labrador had the look of a killer about to attack.

I didn't want to hurt Gus – which would likely bring more trouble – only to save myself. Unfortunately, I'd already shut and locked the door, closing off my best escape route. There was no way I was going to turn my back on an animal that was gathering himself to spring.

So I took the escape route which, according to Fin, I'd been born with. I became a panther and, gathering myself into a crouch, leaped directly towards Gus – but over him, and went up the stairs like climbing a rock-face, in two enormous bounds.

Gus let out a sound between a howl and a whimper, spun round, claws clattering and sliding on the strip of bare wood between the rug and the stairs, and came after me.

I was headed for my room, of course. The only

place inside the house which was mine, my only hope of safety within these walls.

But the door was shut.

Girl-Danni had shut it, of course, before going out last night.

I threw myself at the door, paws up and then raking down. It was a cheap, modern door with a lever-type handle rather than a knob, and the weight of my paws pushed it down even as the impact of my body knocked the door open, and I half-leaped, half-tumbled into the room.

The dog was baying and snapping at my back, but through that fury I must also have heard Claire's voice, pitched high in fear or anger.

I screamed and threw up my hands to protect my face as I fell beneath the dog's weight.

'Gus! Get off!'

The weight was hauled off me. I rolled over and away and when I looked around I saw Claire holding the big black dog by his collar and the scruff of his neck. His forepaws were raised off the ground, but he was still growling.

'Stop that! Bad dog! Bad!' She slapped him on the nose, which had the effect of turning the growl into a whimper.

'What on earth is going on? Danni, are you all right?'

Claire's face was chalk-white except for two burning spots of colour in her cheeks. She was wearing only an oversized pink T-shirt and – I saw, with a nasty jolt of fear – she was holding a shot-gun in the hand that wasn't restraining Gus.

'What happened?' she demanded. 'What's going on? Why are you dressed? Shut up, Gus! Bad dog! Stay!'

'Get him out of here,' I said. My voice came out as a hoarse whisper.

She was still glaring, looking as angry with me as she was frightened, and for a moment I thought she was going to insist on hearing my story before doing anything else, but she must have seen how frightened I was – I was shaking, and hugging myself, still on the floor. There was no way I was going to make any moves Gus might interpret as threatening as long as he was in my room.

Claire's expression changed. 'Are you all right?' No, wait, stay there. I'll lock this creature in the kennel, and then I'll come back.'

When they had gone, I tentatively inspected myself for damage. There were a few grazes and sore spots which might turn into bruises, but Gus hadn't bitten me. The worst damage was psychological: I felt dizzy from so many rapid shifts between human and panther forms. What if I hadn't changed back in time, I thought. What if Claire had come out and seen Gus pursuing a black panther into my bedroom? She'd have shot me, and there'd be bits of dead panther all over the place. Bits of dead *me*.

Neither of the changes had been my choice. The whole thing was out of my control.

It was out of control. I didn't want it any more. I hugged myself harder against the shakes. I couldn't live like this.

I would have stayed crouching on the floor exactly as I was until Claire came back if I hadn't noticed the bed. If Claire saw how I had made it up I'd never talk my way out of trouble. So I scrambled up and had it looking like a bed I might have left only half an hour ago when she returned. I'd also taken off my shoes, and hoped she wouldn't remember I'd been wearing them. Of course she thought it was suspicious that I'd been up and dressed so early, but there was no law against putting on clothes instead of a dressing gown if you happened to wake up early and feel hungry. Anyway, that was the story I was sticking to.

But I needn't have worried too much. It was the strangeness of Gus's behaviour, not mine, that really bothered Claire, especially when she saw the claw-marks on my bedroom door. Naturally it didn't occur to her that they hadn't been made by Gus.

'Oh, Danni, you poor darling! You must have been terrified! I'm so, so sorry!'

'It's not *your* fault.

'Gus has always been, well, friendly to a fault, really. I used to say that if a burglar ever broke in while I was out, Gus would just wag his tail amiably and let him get on with it . . . Although, mind you, he's tremendously protective of *me*. He has growled at people who've come too close to me when he's felt that I was nervous.'

'Maybe he thought I was a threat to you . . .'

'Oh, nonsense!'

'Maybe he blames me for what happened to

Lizzie. I took her out and he never saw her again. He hasn't liked me since then, you know.'

Claire shook her head. 'There's no excuse for his behaviour. He is getting on. Maybe he's getting a bit senile. I'm sure dogs do, just like people. And I've heard they can get mean ... I don't know, maybe he's got a brain tumour or something. I'll take him to the vet, get him checked out. I do hate the thought of having him put down ...'

'Oh, no,' I cried. 'You mustn't! He didn't hurt me.'

'No, but he very easily might have. Look at that door! The sight of it makes me shudder. What on earth was going through his doggy mind? I can't trust him any more.'

'But I'd feel terrible if you had him killed, just because of me!' I felt responsible for Lizzie's death; I couldn't bear to think that Gus, too, should be killed because of what I was.

'It's not just because of you, Danni. If he turned on you, who's to say he wouldn't turn on someone else – possibly a small child.'

'Give him another chance,' I begged. 'Maybe it's just me he doesn't like ... couldn't he stay in the kennel, away from me?'

Claire sighed. 'I got him in the first place because he made me feel safe. Now that's not true. Oh, don't look so tragic! It's not your fault. I won't have him put down unless I absolutely have to. I'll have a word with the vet about him, and he can live in the kennel in the meantime.'

13

The Truth About Cats

Later, we went to church, and Kevin came back with us afterwards. It was raining pretty hard by then, making sailing unappealing, but he was bearing venison steaks for our dinner.

By then I had recovered from the shocks of the early morning, and the mention of venison made me smirk and wish Fin was there to share it. But I didn't feel smug for long.

'We're not the only ones enjoying the deer from the estate,' Kevin said as we sat down to eat.

'Poachers?' asked Claire with interest.

'Erm, no. Not human ones, anyway. We had a stag killed last night – a real prize six-pointer, worse luck – and—'

'I suppose you think it was the panther killed it,' said Claire. Lizzie's death had forced her to change her attitude, but she remained officially sceptical.

'It was certainly killed by an animal, and from the way it was killed and eaten I don't think it could have been anything but a very large and powerful cat. I'd say it was "our panther" – but the thing is, I'm absolutely certain now that there's more than one of them.'

I didn't move. I didn't dare look at him, terrified

that if I did he would look into my eyes and know the truth. I stared at the untouched meal on my plate, and the scent of cooked meat, rising to my nostrils, made my stomach queasy. I couldn't speak, but Claire was there to ask the question for me.

'Come on, Kevin! It's hard enough to believe in one! It's not as if they're native to Britain.'

'There were two kills last night. Two kills that I *know* of, that is. I mentioned the stag. During the same night, probably within the space of a few hours, several sheep were also killed, and by the same method. First thing this morning McWilliams asked me to come out and take a look. Four of his sheep were dead. One had been dragged away and eaten – mostly eaten – but the other three were killed and left to lie. It wasn't need, it wasn't hunger, that made the creature kill them. He killed them out of, I don't know, spite, maybe, or pride. Showing us that he could, and he didn't care if we knew – as if to say he needn't even bother to cover his tracks because we'd never be able to catch him.'

Claire snorted. 'You don't suppose you're being just a wee bit anthropomorphic, do you, Kev, attributing human thoughts and motives to an animal? I seem to remember it was you who cautioned me against doing that very thing when you took me stalking. If those sheep were killed for a nasty, human sort of reason – like, nyah, nyah, can't catch me – isn't it more likely that they were actually killed by a human being? Somebody who'd like us all to think there's a dangerous animal on the loose. Some twisted, unpleasant hoaxer. Animals kill because they have to, because they're hungry or frightened or cornered – not to taunt a farmer.'

'If it was a human, I think he'd have left them all dead but untouched, not carved up one and gone to all the trouble of pretending it had been eaten.'

'Maybe our hoaxer had a hungry dog.'

Kevin sighed, slicing into his steak. 'Why are you so resistant? Why can't you believe in a panther?'

'Why, as soon as I agree there might be one, do you try to convince me there are two?'

'Because there must be. It wouldn't have been possible for one animal to have killed and eaten the stag, then travelled seven miles to wipe out all those sheep – it wouldn't have done something like that, not on a full stomach.'

'But surely a cat wouldn't have done it at all? Not left all those butchered sheep behind?'

'Well . . .' Kevin shrugged. 'It is unusual, but not unheard of. A big cat gets in among penned animals who can't escape, and it goes into a sort of killing frenzy – kills four or five or more, drags one off to eat in safety, and then, once its stomach is full, simply forgets about the others. You don't have to attribute human emotions to the animal to explain what happened last night. But you do, I'm convinced, have to assume that the stag and the sheep were killed by two different animals.'

'So where did the second one come from?'

'I don't know. It might have been here all along, of course. Or maybe it's been driven out of its former territory by overpopulation.'

Claire snorted in disbelief.

'Big cats have been sighted in other parts of Britain,' he reminded her.

'But overpopulation? Come on!'

'Overpopulation in cats doesn't mean the same as it would among people. Except for lions, all cats are solitary hunters, and they have their own territory which they patrol and protect. Even the lowly household moggie has its own territory which it will share only under certain conditions.' He flashed a sudden smile. 'You don't mind if I lecture, do you? Only I've done so much reading on the subject!'

'Go ahead,' said Claire. She glanced at me, half-frowned, then laughed. 'Danni is obviously fascinated – she hasn't touched her food since you started talking!'

'Please, don't let me stop you eating! Anyway, about territories . . . the bigger the cat the larger the territory, generally, but within the species the male and female animals have a rather different approach – female cats will drive off other females, but their territories are smaller and closer together; you might consider them as subjects of a larger male territory. And while a male will tend to fight with another encroaching male, so that only one remains, the other is driven off, he'll accept the presence of any number of female cats within "his" territory, and share the hunting with them. Cats are polygamous. That means,' he said, speaking directly to me, 'One cat has many wives.'

'I thought that was "lives," ' said Claire.

'Sometimes males share,' I objected. I felt slightly

135

breathless, and my heart was beating unpleasantly fast. 'They don't always fight; they can live together.'

'Oh, if you're thinking of domestic cats, I suppose you might get neutered males co-existing, but in the wild . . .'

'What about fathers and sons? Can't they live together?'

'The relationship makes no difference. Younger cats, kittens, of course they're tolerated. But once they reach a certain age, they have to go. If the younger cat doesn't decide of his own accord to strike off in search of his own territory, his own wives, the older male cat might have to make him go. There will have to be a fight, dominance is established, and winner takes all. So our newcomer may have been driven out by his father, or perhaps he was vanquished by an interloper on his own territory.'

'Honestly,' said Claire. 'You'd think this country was seething with panthers. To listen to you, they might be as common as rabbits!'

'Maybe they will be, some day,' said Kevin blandly, forking potato into his mouth. 'If one of our two panthers is a female, they're bound to have cubs, if they haven't already.'

'Maybe they live differently in this country,' I said, a little desperately. 'Maybe they share . . . two males, I mean. Or maybe they have smaller territories. They don't have to fight.'

'Well, that's possible,' Kevin agreed. 'The size of the territory does change according to the availability of game and water. And if there's no female around, two male cats, of whatever species, will often have a sort of wary friendship, or at least a truce, in sharing the same hunting grounds. They don't *have* to fight unless there are females involved, and then they do.'

'Oh, yes, blame the woman,' muttered Claire.

'Now who's anthropomorphizing?' asked Kevin, stumbling slightly over the word. 'It's a matter of instinct. Ever hear of the *Selfish Gene*? All animals are driven to reproduce and to make sure their own genes survive and are passed on. In the case of felines, this means the males want to father as many kittens as possible, which means ensuring that no other male cats will get near any of the females in as large a territory as they're able to protect.'

'So if a female comes into an area that two males are sharing . . .'

'The males have to fight. The winner gets control of the territory, and of the female. And the loser is forced to leave. He's driven away with nothing.'

14

The Fight

On Tuesday I became a student at Mealdarroch Academy. I wasn't nervous about starting at a new school the way I'd been the year before. Then I had worried about being accepted, finding friends, and fitting in, but now there was no point. I knew I would never feel I belonged at Mealdarroch Academy or any other school, but that didn't matter, now I knew I had the animal spirit.

I didn't see Fin until lunch-time that first day, and then he didn't look pleased to see me. He came over to me in the playground, before I had a chance to go into the refectory.

'What are you doing here?'

'Same as you.'

'You're a student here?'

'You might try to look pleased. You did ask me once if I'd consider staying.'

'So you've decided to stay in Scotland?'

I shrugged uncomfortably. 'My folks didn't really give me any choice. What are you thinking? Aren't you pleased?'

'I am,' he said slowly. 'Only . . . it changes things.'

'You mean you think you and the old man are going to fight over me. Well, forget it! That's about the most disgusting thing I've ever heard. As if I'd ever go with him . . . In fact, if you fight, I don't care who wins – I won't go with either of you. I won't be fought over. If you're going to fight, you might as well say goodbye to me now.'

'It's nothing to do with you. We have to fight. I've been avoiding it, keeping out of his way, but it's been coming for a long time. Eventually we'll have a show-down, and one of us will win, and stay, and claim this territory, and the other will have to move on.'

'And I just happen to come with the territory? Well, no thanks. Count me out; I'm not playing.'

'Don't worry about it. I'm young and strong, and I've got more to lose. He wouldn't mind moving on. He might as well; he's just about given up his human life. I know I can take him in a fight. I'm going to win, Danni.'

He put his hand on my shoulder, like I was his already. I pushed it off. 'You don't get it! You're not going to win *me* – nobody is! I'm not a prize to be fought over and won.'

'But we're not talking about *you*, Danni.' He dropped his voice. 'It doesn't matter what you say or how you think you feel about it – none of that matters to the animals. They have their own lives, their own way of living, and we can't control it. Look, we can't talk here.'

Following his glance, I saw we were being watched. I had no idea what Fin's reputation was with the others at the school, or what it would mean for mine to be seen deep in conversation with him, and I didn't really care. But I didn't want to be overheard.

'OK. But when can we talk?'

'Tonight? Usual place.'

'I might be late. I don't know when I can get away.'

He was already moving away, nodding casually. 'See ya.'

I didn't follow him into the refectory. I no longer felt hungry. I couldn't stop thinking of Sunday afternoon's conversation with Kevin about the ways of cats; all that unpleasant, unwanted information jostling in my brain.

I knew that a fight between Fin and the old man must be inevitable, even if I went away. Male cats always did fight, even fathers and sons: it was the way they were made.

'Eventually the younger cat will do something to annoy the old man,' Kevin had said. 'So then he has to go. It's perfectly natural that the young male should leave the land of his mother and his aunties and find his own mate. But to do that, he needs his own bit of land, and that generally means a fight, because there's not enough land to go around. When he leaves his father's territory he has to enter territory patrolled by a different male cat, and so he has to keep moving on until he meets a cat he thinks he can beat – one who is older, or smaller, or younger, or weaker than he is – and then he challenges him. Obviously, this wouldn't apply to panthers in Britain. For them, there's plenty of unclaimed territory, but finding a mate must be a problem.'

'Give me dogs any day,' said Claire. 'Cats are murderous beasts. Baby-killers.'

'But the fathers don't kill their sons, do they?' I asked, with a sick feeling. 'I mean, when it comes to a fight between them?'

'Fights to establish dominance rarely end in death. Claire was talking about something else – when a tom-cat takes over a new territory, the first thing he does is to kill any kittens he finds.'

'Why?'

'Instinct again. That old selfish gene. Each cat wants to ensure the survival of his own genotype. He wants to breed his own kittens, not waste time and energy helping another cat's offspring survive. And once their kittens are dead, the female cats are very soon ready to have more.'

I stared at him in horror. 'Fathered by the cat who killed her babies?'

'I doubt she remembers that for long. Cats aren't human; they don't grieve. Kittens die or grow up and move away, and the role of the female cat is simply to have more, whatever happens.'

'But that's horrible!'

'Life is horrible, if you want to look at it that way. Survival of the species is more important than the survival of individual members of that species. Even for us.' He smiled teasingly. 'If you read much history you'll learn that it's not been unknown for human beings to behave in a similar way, for the same reasons.'

'But cats don't have any choice; humans do,' said Claire, fiercely. It was me she was talking to now, not Kevin, staring at me beadily, making sure I got her message. 'Cats have to act on instinct, humans don't. Human beings can think about their actions and make moral decisions – that's what makes us human. Don't ever forget that. You have a choice.' She gripped my hand. 'You are human; don't forget that.'

Did Claire know?

That was impossible, I decided. Yet she sensed something, a change in me she didn't like, pulling me away from her and her world which had, until recently, been my world, too, and she was trying to warn me against it.

But I shrugged off her warnings. There were things I disliked and things that frightened me about the animal world, but I had never felt completely at home in the human world, and now that I knew why, now that I knew another existence was open to me, I couldn't say no to it.

The idea of staying locked in my room at Fasgadh, locked inside my weak, human body, had no appeal, not when I could feel the panther inside me shifting restlessly, longing for freedom. I wanted freedom, too, no matter if it came trailing strings of danger.

It felt as if Claire was watching me like a hawk, but even hawks sleep. I sat quietly in my room in the dark and listened to the sounds of her going to bed. When the house had been still and quiet for

142

half an hour, then I judged it safe to creep downstairs and outside through the back door.

I really did want to talk to Fin, so I was meaning to go up to the dun as a girl, but by the time I got outside it was midnight and the darkness seemed absolute. A brief, frightened thought, as I approached the fence, of myself stumbling through the woods without even a torch, and then I felt myself flowing and expanding into the night, becoming a part of the dark world around me. It was as a panther that I leaped over the fence separating the garden from the forest, and there, almost immediately, beside the path, I met another.

It wasn't Fin.

The hairs on my back prickled and rose; my ears flattened and I pulled myself slightly back from the stranger.

But he made a low, friendly sound of greeting and stood perfectly still, making no move that could be considered threatening.

After a moment I stepped forward. I felt a warning deep inside, from a place I couldn't identify, and so, although I *knew* he was no threat to me, I was uneasy.

I sniffed delicately at his face and then rubbed mine against his, exchanging scents. Even as I was relaxing into friendship there was still that edgy, nagging worry inside, but now I could identify it as belonging to *her*, the girl, and so I paid it no more attention. *She* was a weak and silly creature, afraid of the dark, quite helpless. Of course she would be afraid of another panther, but I knew I didn't have to be. I knew I had nothing to fear; I knew, from the scent of him and the way he stood, that he wanted to be my friend.

I trotted off into the woods with him. I had been heading up towards the old dun at the top of the hill, but when the older panther nudged me aside, off the path, and then began to trot purposefully in quite a different direction, I hesitated for only a moment. There would be no hunting up at the dun. Whatever called me there could wait. There *would* be hunting with my new friend.

Soon we left the woodland for the open, hilly heath which ran for miles along the coast on both sides of the narrow road. In the darkness, at this late hour, we could run freely in the open, unseen by anyone, yet still we moved from one bit of protective cover to the next, with the caution that had kept us alive through generations.

A rabbit, startled and stupid, bolted across my path. Faster than the thought I was on it, my pounce triggered by the motion. My jaws snapped together at the back of its neck, teeth sinking easily through the flesh and into the vertebrae, breaking its neck in an instant. It was dead before it could scream.

Then, although the saliva was pooling in my mouth and I wanted to eat, I hesitated, and looked at my companion. Although the rabbit was too small, really, for sharing, some deep instinct urged me to offer it.

The eyes of the other met mine, and I lowered my head and dropped the freshly-killed rabbit before him. He brought his face close to the kill, masking it briefly with his whiskers to check for any sign of life, and then he nudged it slightly with his nose, pushing it back towards me, and then retreated, with a graceful motion giving me permission to eat what I had just killed.

And so I ate, while he stood guard. It was only a couple of mouthfuls, but the meat felt good in my stomach, warming me with a glow of energy and well-being.

I had just finished when I felt rather than saw a change in my companion's position and realized just as swiftly that we were no longer alone.

Looking up, I followed his line of vision with my eyes. A dark shape was travelling towards us: another panther.

The panther beside me was as still and rigid as if carved from rock, and the tips of my whiskers tingled with apprehension. I gathered myself and began to sink lower, ready to spring or to run.

Nothing in Fin's posture or relaxed stride showed any awareness of danger or strangeness as he approached. With a weird, low, threatening cry the older panther came to life and leaped at Fin with his claws fully extended.

Fin screamed, his whole body twisted in mid-air and he rolled away. One of his ears was torn and bleeding where the other panther's claws had connected. But he was young and fit; seconds later he was on his feet, on guard, ready to fight.

The two great cats stalked each other, snarling, long tails lashing. They circled each other warily, seeking the advantage, waiting for the best moment to strike hard.

I moaned softly to myself and felt my own tail lash the earth, in imitation of theirs. I was torn between conflicting urges: to run away, or to rush in and try to help Fin. Instinct told me to keep out of it: this was a fight between two males. It was a fight over territorial rights, and I was part of the territory, like it or not.

I didn't like it. At least, the girl I had been didn't like it. As a panther, I wanted only to lie low and keep out of it. It didn't matter who won, it wasn't my fight. But my human nature would keep bubbling up, furious and determined that it did matter to me.

Another yowl of pain from Fin made me flinch, and then I hurled myself against the older panther. It was the most feeble of attacks, because I was fighting myself before I could fight him, but at least I got his attention, which gave Fin a chance to recover.

The old one swiped sideways at me with one heavy paw, and knocked me back on to my haunches. Yet for all its force, the blow had not been meant to do serious damage: he'd retracted his claws and given me the sort of cuff a father might give to a troublesome cub. It wasn't meant to hurt me; it was simply a warning to me to keep out of it before I did get hurt.

Maybe Fin could win this fight on his own, but at what price? I didn't want to risk it. With my help, the odds were suddenly very different. The old one would have to back off. Although I had no experience of fighting, and although every nerve and muscle in my body seemed to scream in protest against what I was making it do, I was young and fit and strong and too reckless for fear.

There was a battle going on inside me very like the one I was watching between the two black cats who grappled together on the ground, rolling, scratching and biting at each other. I saw Fin's blood shining blackly in the darkness, and that sight tore through the last of my resistance, and I rushed forward to help him however I could.

I heard a voice shout, 'Fin!' and stopped still in shock.

Only then did I realize that it was *my* voice; I was standing upright, on two feet. Human emotions had won out over the animal spirit. I cried out in horror.

The two dark shapes in front of me disengaged, leaped up, and shot off in opposite directions. They had run away in fear of me, the human intruder. I had stopped the fight and saved Fin, just as I'd wanted.

Later, maybe, I could be pleased, but just then I was rigid with terror. The darkness was everywhere, suffocating and strange. It seemed to seep into my nose and throat when I tried to breathe. I tried to will myself back into panther form, but even as I tried to believe I could do it, I knew it was a hopeless task. I couldn't think like a panther; I hadn't even been able to do it when I was in a panther's body. Was there some trick to it which I'd forgotten, or had the power, which had been passed to me when the old panther clawed my back, gone away again just as suddenly?

15

Trapped

I didn't know where I was, how far it was to Fasgadh, or in what direction, or even which way to walk towards the road, any road. There was no moon, clouds obscured even the stars, and I could see no light of any kind, anywhere.

I closed my eyes and slowly counted to ten, hoping that when I opened them it would make some difference, but the darkness was still as absolute. As a panther I had seen quite clearly, but now I might as well have been blind.

Fear of running into something, or falling down a hole or off a cliff kept me paralysed at first, but I couldn't bear the thought of just standing, or even sitting, in the middle of nowhere all alone for however many hours it was until morning. There was no one to rescue me if I didn't rescue myself.

So I began to walk. After my first fall on the uneven, rocky ground I slowed my pace to something like a snail's, but still I twisted my ankle, and then bumbled into the painful embrace of a bramble bush. When I'd finally managed to free myself, I shuffled on again, although I was confused now, uncertain that I was sticking to the straight line which I'd tried to imagine for myself, hoping it would lead me down to the road. My arms smarted with a hundred tiny cuts, and soon I was shivering uncontrollably in the chilly night air. Weakly, hating myself for being such a baby, but unable to stop, I started to cry. I would never find my way back to Fasgadh. Long before it got light I would have fallen over and bashed my brains out against a rock.

I stopped and sank down to the ground and hugged my knees to my chest, shivering and sobbing like a lunatic. Maybe it was best to stay in one place until the sky lightened. Yet I didn't feel any safer.

Then, in the dark, something touched me. I heard a hoarse, huffing, coughing sound – the panther's call of greeting – and felt a firm, warm pressure against my leg.

I choked on my tears and my heart leaped. I put out a hand and felt the sleek fur. Fin? I bit my lip rather than say the name aloud, in case it frightened him away – or in case it was wrong. I so wanted it to be Fin, but how could I tell?

The animal turned its great head, almost on a level with mine, and gazed at me with golden eyes, almost the only things I could see in that thick, dark night. The smell of cat filled my nose, frightening me with the intense and conflicting emotions it aroused. I felt both love and fear, gratitude that he had come to me, that he would rescue me, and yet a wrenching sense of loneliness because I was so cut off from this animal who had been my friend that I couldn't communicate with it, couldn't even be sure it was Fin.

Shakily, still, I stood up, resting my hand on the panther's powerful, sleekly-furred shoulder, and I stroked him, gradually moving my hand up until I reached the wounded ear, felt him flinch, felt the blood tacky on fur.

Softly, but more confidently now I knew he was my friend, I said, 'I'm lost. I can't change back – I've tried. Will you take me back to Fasgadh?'

He gave a sort of purring growl which I knew was agreement, and we began to walk. For my sake he went slowly, but, with my hand resting on him, fingers clutching sometimes at the fur, I was able to walk more quickly and confidently through the darkness now. His company transformed the landscape. Although I still couldn't see it, I was no longer afraid. I was half-way home: this was my world, still, around me, even if it was temporarily hidden.

After about twenty minutes I felt the ground change beneath my feet as I stepped down, and realized that we had reached the road. He nudged me in the right direction, and then he left me to walk the rest of the way by myself.

Fin wasn't in school the next day.

I was sure I knew what must have happened, and I didn't like it. There must have been another fight. Once I was safely out of the way the two animals had resumed their battle, and Fin, defeated, had been forced to leave immediately. Or, worse, perhaps he was lying in the woods somewhere with a broken leg, or too weak from loss of blood to move, in either human or animal form. He would die there, with no one to know, no one who could find and help him. Maybe he was dead already. Maybe the old man had gone completely over the top and killed him.

I was frantic. There was no one I could ask, no one I could confide in. I was the only person in the world who might possibly be able to save him, and I didn't know how.

That evening I tried to turn back into a panther – telling myself I must do it, one last time, for Fin's sake – but I just couldn't. It was like the first time I'd tried, on the hillside with Fin, when it had seemed impossible, and, when I thought about it, I suspected that I was failing now for the same reason I'd failed then, and that reason was that I didn't want it enough. I wanted to change for Fin's sake, but what about my own? I wanted to be strong and swift and free; I didn't want to be a creature ruled by instinct, to find my loyalty to Fin could be wiped out at the swipe of a paw, making me the subservient mate of someone my human self hated and feared.

I couldn't do it. I couldn't let go of my human feelings, my human self. I didn't want to be an animal, but a girl inside a panther skin. And that wasn't the gift of the animal spirit. While I was so divided, I could not change. The magic had left me, and I felt as if it had been taken away, although it was my own refusal to be an animal which trapped me where I was.

Fin wasn't at school again the next day. I looked

for him all morning, but by lunchtime had to admit to myself that I hadn't just missed seeing him – he really wasn't there. That was when I really felt despair. I hadn't realized until then that I'd nearly convinced myself his absence of the day before wasn't really significant – that he'd overslept, or had gone to the doctor to get his ear attended to. But two days in a row – that was serious.

Claire met me at the school gates that afternoon, intercepting me before I could head for the bus.

'Hi,' she said, with a nervy, forced brightness, 'I finished my work early today, so we can go home together!'

My heart sank. It really was as if she sensed my plans and then moved to block them. I'd made up my mind to start searching for Fin. The very least I could do would be to go up to the dun, and if I couldn't change shape, I had to go out while it was still light. With Claire around, I hadn't a hope of getting out of the house unseen.

I did my best.

'I need to go for a walk. I need to think about things.'

'Think indoors. It's not safe out there.'

I shook my head at her and tried to scoff. 'I can't believe I'm hearing this from you!'

She gave me a bitter look. 'I had to change my mind. Circumstances changed it for me. After what happened to Lizzie and you I'm surprised you can even think of going out.'

'I'll stay on the road,' I lied. 'I won't go far. Honestly, I'm sure I'll be perfectly safe. I'd have to be awfully unlucky to be attacked twice . . . I'm sure the panther must be miles away by now.'

'Oh, no, it's not,' she said grimly.

My spine prickled and I stared at her.

'Look,' she said. 'I didn't want to upset you, or worry you, but . . . you have to know. I saw it yesterday, actually in the garden. It wasn't completely dark and I could see it quite clearly. It was sitting on that big rock by the fir tree, and it was watching the house. I'm sure it was watching the house.

'Anyway, I've brought Gus inside. He's just not safe in that kennel, not from a killer like that. He's in the kitchen just now, but I'll have him in my bedroom at night, keep him out of your way.'

'That's all right,' I said. I was trying to come to grips with this new information. Was the old one looking for me? Or was it possible that the panther Claire had seen was Fin? Could it be that, just as I was stuck in my human body, Fin now was trapped inside the panther's skin? It might work both ways; certainly, part of my fear of changing was the fear that I wouldn't be able to change back.

'What—' but I stopped myself before I asked her what the panther had looked like – as if she could have told me! 'What happened, after you saw him?'

'It looked back at me, bold as brass. It was almost as if it *wanted* to be seen. Anyway, I went for my gun. But by the time I'd loaded it and got to the back door, the creature had gone. But, you see, it's out there. It will come back. It hasn't gone away.' She gripped my arm and stared fiercely into my eyes. 'We're not safe, either of us. Don't you start thinking you're safe anywhere outside, not even in the garden, not even in broad daylight. We won't be safe until it's dead.'

The next day, Friday, Fin was back at school.

I almost didn't recognize him. He had a new, very short haircut and a bandage over his ear, and he was wearing brand-new jeans, boots, and a spotlessly white polo shirt. But the biggest change of all was in himself. If his clothes were bright and new, he seemed to have faded. He wore a blank, shutdown expression on his face, and even the way he walked was different. I had never before known that the way someone moved could speak so clearly of unhappiness.

He didn't try to talk to me. When I saw him in the halls and called out his name, his only response was a kind of wincing away, and he wouldn't meet my eyes.

What on earth was going on?

I had to force myself on him, practically grab him, in the playground at lunch-break. 'What happened to you? Where've you been?'

'Don't you know?'

'Oh, sure, that's why I'm asking. Do you think I'm psychic? I've been worried about you, Fin! I didn't know where you were, or what had happened.'

'She didn't tell you, then.'

'She? Do you mean Claire? What's she got to do with it?'

'She put the social services onto me, right enough. They'd been looking for the old man, but nobody's seen him for yonks. They only caught me because I turned up for school. And when they saw what he'd done to my ear—' he shook his head. 'I couldn't deny he'd done it, only that it wasn't like they thought. I would've done the same, or worse, to him, if I'd had the chance. Only I didn't catch up with him again after I left you that night, and now I never will.'

He was talking as if to himself, not meeting my eyes.

'So where did they take you? Where've you been the past two days?'

'First, the Mid-Argyll to get me ear stitched up, and get jabs. Then away for interviews, and to get kitted out with new clothes while they tried to figure out what to do with me.'

'But they let you come back,' I said, trying to work out why he was so miserable. 'They didn't put you in a home.'

Now he looked right at me, and hostility sparked in his dark eyes. 'They did so! I'm only staying in Mealdarroch because the teachers say I'm doing well, and there's a family does fostering have agreed to take me.'

'Are they nice? Where are you staying?'

He wrinkled his nose. 'They're nosy and bossy – they think that means they care. I can't move without they ask me where I'm going. The house – it's that big black and white one by the quay, just next to the craft shop, you know it? – the house is full of people. I have to share a bedroom with another boy.'

'Well, it sounds better than the caravan, at least.'

'Oh, aye, running water and a flush toilet and all my meals. But there's a price to be paid for that, you know. They've taken away my freedom.' He looked me in the eye, no longer hostile, simply wretchedly unhappy. 'The old man didn't beat me, but he's won, thanks to them. He gets to keep his territory. I'll have to go away.'

'But I thought you said . . . is it just temporary? Won't they let you stay?'

'It's not *them*,' he said, exasperated. 'It's nothing to do with what they want – it's what *I* want. Don't you understand? They've taken away my territory, and given me clean clothes and regular meals instead. I might as well be in a zoo. If I stay, I lose half of my life, keep the animal spirit in a cage, try to pretend I'm just a boy. I can't do that. I won't do that.'

'But – surely, if you're going to school, during the school term, you can't be out running through the woods and hunting all night as well!'

'Not every night, no. I made that choice for myself – the old man couldn't see the point of it, staying in most nights so I'd be able to go to school. But I think once upon a time he must have done the same, must have spent a lot more time as a man, with a job, a real, daytime life. Only I guess as he got older and drifted away from the places where people had known him, he kind of stopped seeing the point of being human. He was moving that way

157

when he met me. He was finding it harder and harder to get by in the world as a man. There wasn't any work for him, there weren't people who cared what he did. It was easier to get his meals by hunting and find himself a den on the hillside than it was to find jobs that would earn money that he could turn into food and shelter. I think he only went on making any effort at all because of me. And finally he gave up. He doesn't want to be a man any more, at all.'

'But you don't want to stop being human.'

'No,' he agreed. 'I don't. I like having two lives – I don't want to give up either one. I just want to be left alone to lead my life as I want to – both my lives. But they won't let me. They're forcing me to choose. I'll have to run away.'

If Fin ran away, I'd have no one. When you've never had something, they say you don't miss it. But to lose something really hurts. I'd lost the animal spirit; I couldn't bear to lose my only friend as well. I couldn't think what to say, so I just blurted out my other loss.

'I can't change any more. I tried – I was going to go and look for you – and I couldn't!'

'Don't be daft,' he said wearily.

'It's true!'

'If you aren't changing it's because you don't really want to.'

'I *do* want to. Only . . . maybe not without you. I was afraid the old one had hurt you really badly, maybe even killed you.'

He snorted. Something of his old look was

coming back despite the new clothes and haircut. 'No way! If we have another fight, I'll take him for sure.'

'Claire's seen a panther watching the house.'

'Aye, he will be, now I'm away.'

'Waiting for me?'

He nodded. 'He shouldn't be letting *her* see him, though. He should know better than that. But maybe he doesn't any more. Now he's not a man any more, there may be things he's forgotten.'

'Could that be why he killed all those sheep?'

'What sheep?'

I realized it had been a very long time since I had spoken to Fin. 'Kevin said a panther slaughtered a lot of sheep the same night we brought down that stag. It sounded more a human thing, to kill so much more than he could possibly eat.'

'He'll get himself shot, carrying on like that.'

'Fin, could you make him go away? I mean, are you sure that you could beat him in a fight?'

'Don't you think I could?'

'It's just that I wouldn't want to ask you to do something that – well, it would be my fault if you got hurt.'

'Of course it wouldn't be your fault. Anyway.' His shoulders slumped. 'I'm not going to get a chance. I can forget about running free as long as I'm here.'

'Oh, come on, Fin, you must be able to sneak away sometimes! I did it. They don't chain you to your bed, do they?'

'No, they don't – but they don't give me a room

to myself, either. You haven't got a roommate who wets his bed and sleepwalks. They've told me it won't always be like this, he's going through a bad patch just now, but this bad patch means he's up two or three times in the night, and there's always people coming in and out. The first time they see my bed empty and I'm nowhere in the house – well, I might as well not come back, because then they *will* lock me up. You don't know how easy you've got it, with only your godmother to worry about.'

It was his talking about my situation which gave me the idea. 'Would they let you go away for the weekend? Would they let you stay with us? Claire would say yes, I'm sure she would. She's been wanting to meet you, and there's plenty of room. And then it'll be easy for you to sneak out at night, and run up to the dun, just like old times.'

I saw the hope flare in his face, although he tried to damp it down. 'They probably won't let me, they'll say it's too soon or something.'

'Well, ask them! No, I know – even better. We'll get Claire to ask them. I'm sure they know her; they'll probably be pleased to have one less for dinner. And she won't take no for an answer. Come on, we have to try.'

16

Death of a Panther

Claire was delighted to help 'your poor young friend', and she knew his foster parents well enough, and so it was arranged for Fin to spend all of Saturday, and Saturday night, and Sunday, with us at Fasgadh. We were to meet him in Mealdarroch on Saturday morning, where Kevin was to take the two of us out for a sail while Claire attended to some newspaper business.

I hadn't expected Fin to be keen – I'd thought he'd see a whole day in adult company as something to be suffered through to get what he really wanted. But he turned out to know Kevin, and to be a knowledgeable sailor. Although he wasn't a regular member of the sailing club, he had been out with them occasionally, and learned to sail. He'd even been on Kevin's boat before.

I was surprised, seeing Fin in a different light. He wasn't exactly the boy I'd imagined, slipping anonymously through his days, uninvolved in local life, living only for the night and his secret animal life. I wasn't his only friend. I felt a pang of jealousy, and I had to question my earlier notion that it was the animal spirit which cut me off from everyone else. Maybe that was just an excuse. Maybe, if I let it, I'd be headed down the road the old man had taken, where finally it became too much trouble to be human. Fin knew he didn't want that, yet if he ran away, how much choice would he have? As I began to realize how much Fin would be giving up if he ran away and how desperate he must be to consider it, it was no longer only for selfish reasons that I promised myself I would do whatever I could to help him stay.

That wasn't the only thing I learned that day.

Kevin said he'd like to have a quiet word with me about 'this panther Claire claims to have seen.'

I looked him in surprise. 'But you've seen it!'

He sighed. 'Yes. I don't doubt the panther exists. Only, Claire does go to extremes. First she doesn't believe in it at all, then it's watching the house – stalking her. I've tried telling her that panthers don't operate like that. If it was stalking her she'd never know it – certainly it wouldn't be hanging about the house, letting her see it.'

'It let me see it, too,' I said. 'I saw it from my window. It was in the garden, and it looked up at me for a long time before it ran away. This was ages ago – I didn't say anything because I knew Claire wouldn't believe me. But she's right: it *is* watching the house.'

Kevin gave a low whistle. He was silent for a little while, thinking. The only sounds were those made by the wind in the sail and the slap of the water against the sides of the boat as it moved smartly along under Fin's control. Then he said, 'It's not behaving like a panther should. But then that sheep-killing business wasn't normal, either. It could mean trouble. Don't tell your godmother, Danni, because I don't want to alarm her more than she is already, but it's a good job she's got a gun and knows how to use it. And I guess having the motion detector installed wasn't such a daft idea as I thought.'

'What motion-detector?'

'She had an electrician come out yesterday – I expect it was while you were at school – to install outside lights, front and back, which would be triggered after dark by anything moving past. I told her those things could be a real nuisance, set off whenever the wind blew some branches in the wrong direction, or a stray dog or a deer happened to be passing through, but maybe she had the right idea. Certainly a panther prowling around the house would set it off, and a floodlit garden would take away its natural advantage.'

I looked at Fin, I couldn't help it. But if it had occurred to him that sneaking out of Claire's house tonight wasn't going to be the doddle I'd said it would be, his face gave nothing away.

Later, when we were alone, supposedly watching television while the adults cooked and drank wine in the kitchen, he told me why he wasn't worried. 'Lights can be switched off. You just have to find out where the switch is.'

'And what if she checks it later? After we've gone to bed – after she *thinks* we've gone to bed? And turns it back on?'

He shrugged. 'What if she does. So she sees me.'

'Fin, she's got a gun, and she'll use it!'

'Not on me, she won't. Don't worry, I'll be too fast for her. I'll be running. Look, it's not me who's been sitting and staring up at the house, daring her to shoot! If he's mad enough to *want* to be shot . . .'

'Maybe he doesn't know she had a gun.'

'He doesn't have to know. You never assume a human is harmless; you keep out of their way, always.'

'Like you,' I said. 'Running alongside the car, letting me see you.'

He scowled. 'That was different.'

'How?'

'I'd've been away like a shot if the car had stopped or if you'd even wound down your window . . . it wasn't such a risk. Anyway, if I hadn't done it, I'd never have known about you – and neither would you.'

'But it's because of *him* that I changed.' I bit my lip. The old man terrified me, yet I couldn't forget how I'd felt when we'd both been panthers, and he had been my friend. 'I don't want him killed. I just wish he'd go away.'

'Don't worry, he will. And then Claire will settle down and we can forget the floodlights and the gun. And then you'll see, you'll be able to change. You could now, if you weren't frightened. Speaking of frightened, what's with your godmother?'

'Anyone would be frightened if a panther was prowling around their house all the time. She has no way of knowing it's after *me*, not her.'

164

'I don't mean that. I mean the way she is with us.'

'Us?'

'Me. You. At first I thought maybe it was because I was a stranger in the house, but she looks at you the same way. She's scared of you.'

I stared in astonishment and then laughed uncertainly. But he wasn't joking. 'No, she's not! How could she be? Why should she be?'

He shrugged. 'I don't know. That's what I'm asking. Because she is. You can sense it – well, I can. Maybe you haven't had enough practice. But it's not something I'm mistaken about. Sometimes, some people get a whiff of the animal – usually it's when I've just changed back. You have to learn to be careful about it, because it can lead to trouble, when people sense you're different. Sometimes they're frightened; more often, they get aggressive.'

'Claire's not afraid of me! She's kind of odd and nervy, I know, but she's very fond of me – she's said so.'

'I never said she wasn't fond of you.'

I stood up suddenly. 'I'd better go see if tea's ready.'

Walking towards the kitchen, I didn't intend to eavesdrop, but Claire spoke loudly, her voice carrying into the hall, and I walked especially lightly these days.

'He comes every night,' Claire was saying. 'If you stay and keep watch with me, you'll see for yourself. In fact, I'd be grateful if you would stay – I could use a back-up. I think he's trying to lure me outside, and I suppose I will have to go out, to get a clear shot at him, but I'd feel safer if there was someone else keeping me covered. We might be able to get him tonight.'

I went into the kitchen. 'You're not going to shoot him!'

She didn't even look up. 'We're talking about the panther.'

'Why do you want to kill him?'

She stared at me. 'Look, Danni, this isn't some Bambi creature for you to get all soppy about! It's a killer. It killed my dog and if I don't do something about it, it might kill you and me, too. Doesn't that bother you at all?'

'Well, but, do you have to shoot him? Couldn't you set a trap? There might be zoos that would want a black panther—'

She laughed shortly. 'A trap? What kind of a trap? Are you proposing I dig a tiger-pit in my garden? Somehow, I don't think it would work. I don't think this old fellow would be easily caught. Anyway, I don't want to catch him. I want to kill him.'

'Couldn't you wait . . .' I was desperate. It wasn't just the thought of her killing the old man which upset me – although I knew it would be murder, and she didn't – but that she might shoot Fin instead.

'Wait for what?'

'He might go away—'

'He's not going to go away.'

'Then there's no hurry, is there? You could shoot

166

him any time. Couldn't you wait until some other night – when I *don't* have company?'

'Oh, I see, you think I'll embarrass you in front of your friend!' She laughed without humour. 'Kevin, will you kindly inform this young lady that I am what is known as a crack shot. There's no chance of a stray bullet hitting your friend or anything except the big cat I aim at.'

'I'll hang on till gone ten,' said Kevin. 'If the cat shows up before then, you can have a shot at him and I'll back you up. If he hasn't shown by then, you'll wait for another night.'

She looked unhappy, and he said, teasingly, 'No good comes from looking out of your windows after ten o'clock at night'

Claire snorted. 'I'll look out my windows whenever I choose. It's one of the joys of living in the country. If I can't sleep, or I wake up for some reason, I often look out. Once I saw a couple of hares, dancing on the lawn. Another time I saw a badger. And more deer come through the garden than you'd think.'

'Well, you'll know all about it with your new light,' said Kevin.

He stayed as he had said he would until nearly half-past ten, and throughout the evening there was no sign of the panther, although, after about nine o'clock, the new floodlights snapped full on three different times – never for any reason we could work out.

'Oh, do we have to have the lights on all night?' I asked, using my most whining voice. 'I just know I won't be able to sleep with a searchlight glaring into my window every ten minutes!'

To my surprise, Claire agreed. Maybe she felt embarrassed because the panther hadn't shown up when she'd been so sure he would, or maybe she decided she didn't really want to know if he turned up later. Or maybe my whine was especially effective that evening. Anyway, the new lights were switched off, Kevin drove away in his Land Rover saying he'd see us in church the next day, and Fin and I went upstairs, supposedly to bed.

I told Fin he'd better give it another hour or more, to wait until Claire was asleep, but he shook his head.

'I'll go out your window. With that tree out there I can get back just as easily as long as you leave it open.'

I was reluctant to let him go, and he sensed it. 'You could come with me.'

I looked at the window and tried to imagine it, but I could feel that fatal hesitation, a deep resistance, inside me. 'No, I can't.'

'Don't keep saying that, or you'll start to believe it. If you don't *want* to—'

'I *do* want to – but I'm afraid!' I bit my lip. 'And if you're going to fight, I don't think I could just stand back and watch.'

'Then you're right to stay in. I'll see you later.'

He turned away from me, towards the window, and it was as if a shadow fell across him: darkness gathered at that end of the room, and then darkness solidified in the form of a great black cat which leaped up, gathered itself on the window-sill, then sprang out and down and away from the house.

I went to the window to watch him go. There was a painful yearning in my chest, but I couldn't follow him; I couldn't even see him now, with my weak human eyes, in the darkness. A deep, frantic barking started up – Gus, exiled in his kennel, must have caught the alien scent. Seconds later, light was glaring everywhere, and I knew Claire must have switched on the new lights. But by then, of course, Fin was long gone, and the thought of Claire peering out into the garden, perhaps even clutching her gun, didn't worry me. After five or ten minutes the lights went out, and I got ready for bed.

The sound of a gunshot woke me.

My feet hit the floor before I even knew I was awake. Heart pounding, mouth dry, terrified, I threw open my bedroom door. There was the sound of another explosive shot, horribly close, as I reached the hallway, and I ran for the stairs.

Just before I reached the bottom, Claire came out of her bedroom, carrying a gun.

'Get back up here,' she called sharply, seeing me. 'Go back into your room.'

I stopped. 'Somebody's out there shooting.'

'That was me,' she said crisply. 'Through the bedroom window. It was a straight shot.' Her lips thinned in a smile of triumphant. 'I got him.'

My stomach lurched. 'What? Got who?'

'The panther.' She came down the stairs. 'I'm pretty sure I killed him, but I need to make sure. I definitely hit him, but if he's still alive, I'm not going to leave him in agony. But it's risky – he could be shamming, or badly hurt – and I really can't cover both of us, so you must stay inside.' As she spoke, she unlocked the door.

'You killed him?'

'I certainly hope so. Now, don't start! I want you to—'

But I didn't wait to hear what she wanted. I was terrified in case it was Fin she'd killed. The door was open, and I ran through it.

'Danni! No! Don't be daft!' The tips of her fingers brushed my shoulder as she lunged, but she could not hold me back.

It was that dim, murky hour just before dawn, when everything looks grey and shadow-shrouded, but the night is beginning to lift. Even in that unhelpful non-light, even with my weak human eyes, I had no trouble finding the panther: it lay like a pool of black water on the grass.

Although I couldn't tell if it was Fin or the old man, one of them was dead. My mouth stretched open and a howl of rage and grief erupted. In a way it didn't matter who it was; one of my own kind was dead.

But there was no time for mourning, not here and now. This place wasn't safe.

I don't know exactly when I changed, but as I began to run for my life, it was with the speed and the power of the panther that I was.

17

A New Life?

I went sailing over the low wire fence, out of the garden, into the relative safety and concealing gloom of the forest. Muscles pulling and bunching effortlessly, I loped up the long hillside to the dun. If he was still alive, Fin would be certain to return to his den some time before dawn.

The familiar scent of him, everywhere about the dun, was comforting, but the freshest traces were several hours old, and there was no other sign of him. I prowled restlessly, wary of staying too long in one place in case the humans should track me down, yet reluctant to leave without making contact with Fin, if he was still alive.

As a human I would have brooded and worried endlessly about him, imagining him dead or badly hurt, but as a cat I was simply uneasy, and my own skin was my main concern.

And yet, almost as strong as the instinct for self-preservation which urged me to run and hide before the woman with a gun could find and shoot me, too, was another emotion, and it had to be expressed even if it put me in danger.

Crouching on top of the pile of ancient stones, I raised my head and let out a low yet carrying cry.

And he heard me.

The clouds above me were just beginning to glow with a faint, pearly light. The cry might almost have been an echo, but I knew it was not, I knew it had come from Fin.

Moments later I saw him coming, weaving his way through the dying bracken and the clumps of heather and broom. His posture was relaxed, his long tail eloquent: I knew by the sight of him that he'd had a good evening's hunting, and that he didn't know about the old one's death.

I leaped down from the wall and ran to him, brushing my face against his, urgently. He sensed my distress, but not the reason for it. But my concern for his safety communicated, more quickly than words could have, my conviction that we would not be safe here, and, as immediately, he accepted this, and we were away, running together through the dawning.

We kept away from the roads to travel deeper inland and upland, gradually ascending *Beinn Dubh*, the highest hill in the area. As we ran past a couple of silly, bleating sheep, one of the creatures nearly broke its own neck trying to get away. They would have been easy kills, but I felt urgently that any delay could be fatal – especially a delay which signposted our direction as a carcass would have.

Near the summit of Beinn Dubh was a cave. As we entered it, my nose told me that Fin had come here before, and so had the old one. The scent brought with it a rush of powerful emotions, and abruptly I found myself on two legs, a girl again, shivering in pyjamas, the ground cold beneath my bare feet.

'What happened?' asked Fin, who had changed when I did, probably driven by the same need I felt, to talk as only humans could.

'Claire shot the old one. He's dead.'

He gave a sigh as if he'd been punched, and leaned back against the wall of the cave. I felt unhappily removed from him. As animals, although I hadn't been able to tell him exactly what was wrong, we had shared our feelings, we had understood each other in a way that, now, we could not. I wished I could rub my face against his, but the very idea of doing such a thing made me go hot with embarrassment. I couldn't even touch him, not knowing if he would welcome it, not knowing if it would be any sort of comfort. Life could be so simple, but human thoughts tangled everything up in knots.

'I was afraid that it might have been you – that she might have seen you when you were coming back.'

'But you changed?'

'I didn't plan it, it just happened. I wanted to get away, that was all, I wasn't thinking – oh!' My heart lurched.

'What?'

'I think maybe Claire saw me change. She was right behind me, and it was dark, but not *that* dark. I didn't even think about that, I was just trying to get away. Oh, no.'

Fin shook his head. 'Don't worry about it. Even if she saw you, she wouldn't believe her own eyes.

She just couldn't. This is the woman who refused to believe there could be a panther in Scotland until one killed her dog.'

'Well, she's a believer now.'

'Yeah, and she killed the one she believed in. Oh, what difference does it make what she saw? You'll go back to her and convince her it never happened, yeah?'

'I don't know. Maybe I won't go back at all.' It was mostly bravado, saying that. I didn't stop to think what it might mean – I just wanted Fin to know I was on his side, and words were all I had.

And it worked. He looked fractionally less gloomy. 'Yeah? You'd do that? You'd stay with me?'

I nodded, suddenly uncomfortable. 'We should stay together, don't you think? I mean, we're like family. There's nobody else like us. Nobody else knows what it's like.'

He yawned suddenly, hugely, as naturally as a cat. 'I need a kip, how about you?'

It was easier, safer, and of course much more comfortable to sleep as cats, lying on our sides in the cave, curled together, warm and safe. As a girl, I'm sure I would have been awake for hours, fretting about what would happen next, but once I was a cat, all human concerns dropped away, and I was able to slip easily into a restful sleep.

We slept away the day. As we emerged from the cave in the late afternoon we saw the first search parties, far away in the distance, combing the hills for us.

We didn't have to discuss what to do. They were looking for two children, and as animals whose second nature it was to stay unseen, we had a definite advantage over them. For a little while longer we watched the distant figures crawling over the dun atop that lower hill, and then we left them to it, in favour of our own search for food.

But the group we'd spotted at the dun was not the only search-party out that day. The scent of human-kind was everywhere, and the ring of human voices disturbing the peace of the land. Once, I heard my own name, and the sound of it struck me like a whiplash, stinging, making me leap away in fright.

The humans were noisy, intrusive and slow. They gave ample warning of every move they were about to make, so that even when they came closest – once, a searcher passed within inches of my nose – we were able to hide ourselves.

But although we could hide, we couldn't hunt with so many people about. Even after night had fallen and the searchers had left, the deer had been thoroughly spooked, and we had no chance of getting anywhere near a potential kill. Almost by accident, Fin caught a bird. It was too small to share, and I doubt it made the slightest bit of difference to his hunger.

I began to think about the sheep we'd seen much earlier on the side of Beinn Dubh, and my mouth began to water. I knew Fin avoided killing sheep because he didn't want to give farmers reason to come after him, but the need for caution really didn't count for much against the hunger in my belly.

We had split up, hoping to better our chances, and the path I was on, travelling back towards the dun, wasn't likely to bring me within the reach of any sheep, although I'd hoped there might be deer. As I paused to consider changing direction, wondering about my chances, I caught the whiff of woodsmoke.

I traced its direction with nose and whiskers. It was coming from the dun.

Caution should have made me keep away, but curiosity sent me slinking silently closer, right up to the very wall of the dun. It was another dark night; I trusted in the darkness and my own silent agility to keep me hidden as I leapt lightly up onto the wall and looked down.

There within the centre of the semi-circular wall, at the heart of what was left of the old, stone-built fortress, huddled out of the wind beside a small fire, sat Claire. I looked everywhere for someone else, but she was all alone, without even her dog beside her. Her only companion was her gun, lying close at hand, the barrel gleaming faintly, evilly, in the firelight.

I hunched down, gathering myself. She was not unprotected, but neither was she protected. The gun could only save her if she understood the danger she was in quickly enough to snatch it up and aim before I came down on top of her and broke her neck. And it was very unlikely that she would be able to do that now that I was in killing range.

There below me was my prey.

There below me was my godmother.

Two absolutely conflicting needs, two different minds, pulled me in opposite directions. The one was hungry, focused and practical. It wanted to survive, and to do that, it must eat. The other was unspeakably horrified by the idea that Claire could be food. No matter how angry I might be with her, no matter even if I disliked her, we were alike, we were connected, as all members of the same species were. If I killed Claire – if I killed and ate *any* human being – I would be denying my own humanity, cutting myself off from it. I would be for ever lost, on my own, a species apart.

And as I realized that, I suddenly wondered if the old man had faced this same moment of decision, and chosen differently from me. Had he killed someone? Was that what had finally changed him from a human with the animal spirit into an animal?

I shifted slightly on the wall, preparing to turn and jump down the way I had come, but my thoughts, too human, must have made me careless. I dislodged a stone or made some other small noise which alerted Claire.

Just below me, she looked around and struggled to her feet.

'Danni?'

Her voice was wavering and frightened. I should have fled the instant she moved – a real panther would never have looked back. But I did, caught in that moment between two states of existence, and as I looked, something I saw in Claire's eyes froze me in astonishment.

I heard her gasp, saw her edge sideways, never taking her eyes from mine, groping for her gun.

Before she could put her hand on it I'd twisted round and leaped away, off the wall, away from Claire, into the night, scrambling down the steep hillside into the sheltering dark of the forest.

Sometimes I went on four legs, sometimes on two, staggering and hobbling painfully on bare feet. I was so shaken by what had happened to me, by what I now knew, and so weakened by hunger and weariness, that I lost track of who or what I was sometimes. It was morning by the time I made my way back to the cave at the top of Beinn Dubh, and Fin was waiting for me, dark purplish stains around his mouth.

'Have you eaten?'

I shook my head.

'Come here.' He led me to a bramble bush. 'They'll no fill you up, but they're better than nothing.'

They certainly were. I crammed handfuls into my mouth, shaking a little, scratching my arms, pricking my fingers, and consuming a few small worms and flies as well in my eagerness. I started to feel a bit better, and then I told Fin about seeing Claire.

'And, Fin, you'd never guess – she's one of us! She has the animal spirit!'

'Never.'

'I saw it! It was shining out of her eyes, just like you said. Well, I didn't really know what you meant, when you said it, but I did when I saw it. I knew.'

'Well, so, but,' he said, and sighed. 'And will you tell her? I think she'll no thank you – I think she'll no believe – sure she won't.'

I hadn't thought about telling her. I hadn't thought about any practical use of my knowledge. It was just there, the knowledge, and somehow hugely important. It changed my perception of Claire and my feelings about her. 'I ought to tell her, whether she believes me or not. I mean, she ought to know. It's only fair, don't you think?'

He shook his head. 'She doesn't *want* to know. Could be someone has tried to tell her before . . . or maybe she's felt the animal spirit inside herself, only she thinks it's not a power, but a curse. Now it makes sense that she was scared of us.'

'If she's scared it's because she doesn't understand. I think not-knowing might have been her problem all along. She feels at home in the country, and she's drawn to animals without knowing why. And she's felt a special connection with me from the time I was born.' I remembered her refusal to go stalking, and wondered if maybe, while hunting the deer, she'd felt the stirring of the hungry animal inside, and if that had been what had frightened her into giving up the sport. 'It all makes sense! Oh, Fin, I have to tell her. What she does with it is up to her, but I can't make that decision for her. It's just not fair that I know and she doesn't.'

'So you're going to go back because you think you owe it to her to tell her something she doesn't want to know about herself?'

The bramble bush was pretty much exhausted. I gave up the search and wiped my hands on my by now utterly ragged pyjamas. I suddenly felt nervous. 'That's not why.'

'You never meant to come with me at all, did you? Well,' he shrugged. 'Suit yourself. I'll be all right on me own.'

'We're both going back.'

He shook his head.

'Oh, Fin, be sensible! You can't stay here – you'll starve!'

He snorted. 'One bad night and you think you're starving! You don't know you're born! There's plenty of game; I'll have better luck tonight. If that's all that's worrying you ... we wouldn't stay *here*, of course. We'd move on, somewhere we wouldn't have to spend our days playing dodge the search party.'

'And what would we do in the new place? Live wild? The whole time? In the winter?'

'What do you think those fur coats are for, then?'

'You mean – we'd stop being human?'

He looked uneasy and he scowled. 'Not for ever.'

'But you'd give up half your life, at least for awhile – you'd be a panther all the time. Would that be better than having to be a boy all the time?'

'I can be human whenever I want, as long as I'm free. But I can't be a panther in somebody else's house where they're watching me all the time.'

180

'There's not much point to being a boy all by yourself in the heather, with nowhere to live, nothing to eat, nothing to wear and no one to talk to, is there? You say it's not for ever, but how do you know? It could be that once you start you'd forget how to change back – or you'd forget why you ever wanted to, and end up like your old man.'

'I don't think so.'

I felt despairingly that I was about to lose the only friend I'd ever had. He would leave me, just as my mother had, for a life where I did not belong. 'Please stay.'

'Come with me.'

'Fin, I can't live like that!'

'You can.'

'All right then, I don't want to. I don't want to give up my human life – and I don't think you want to, either. Otherwise, you'd have done it long ago. You've got more to lose than I have – my folks just dumped me here, with somebody I don't especially get on with, but you've made friends, people who would miss you if you disappeared. And you're good at school, which I've never been. Your teachers think you're pretty special, I've heard. Me, I'm no good at anything; I might as well drop out now.'

'Don't be daft.'

'Oh, you think I should continue my education in the woods? How? Panthers don't read.'

'You don't talk like somebody who's no good at school.'

'I like to read. I have a good vocabulary. But that's all. Maths is pure torture.'

'Maths is a doddle.'

'I can't understand the first thing about it.'

'I could show you—' he stopped and set his jaw.

'But you won't stay.'

'I can't!'

'You can.'

'All right then: I don't want to. I won't live in a cage. Don't you understand what would happen to me if I went back now? They'd lock me up. Runaway kid equals trouble. Probably they'd send me away to some "secure accommodation" which might as well be a prison, probably in a town. I can't live like that; it would kill me.'

'It would kill me, too,' I said. 'Oh, Fin, I don't think it will be that bad, honestly! We'll find a way to go on being what we are. Maybe Claire will help us, once she knows – don't worry, I'm not going to rush into telling her, I don't want to panic her – but she does have the animal spirit. The three of us have that in common – it's something special, and we should stick together.'

His expression had changed, become more distant, and I realized I'd made a mistake by bringing Claire into the argument. He hardly knew her; he certainly felt no bond with her, and she'd just killed his old man.

'I don't need you,' he said. 'Cats are solitary beasts.'

I almost walked away from him then, in terrible pain because he didn't want me. But luckily I hesitated, and as I stared at him, realized that his posture, his body language, was saying something completely at odds with his words. He was in pain, just as I was. And he didn't want me to go.

So I said, 'But people aren't. I need you.'

His shoulders relaxed, and I knew I'd reached him.

'What are we going to tell them, if we go back?' he asked.

'Oh, I don't know . . . let's work out a story. You never ran away – I did. And you came after me and found me.'

'If they try to lock me up, I'll run away for sure.'

'If they try to lock you up, I'll go with you. Hmmm, maybe we should make you a hero – I could say you saved my life!'

'I did, and all,' he said. 'I showed you where the brambles were. You'd have starved to death, else.'

I laughed with relief, and finally he smiled. I was so pleased then, so happy I hardly knew how to show it. I went over and rubbed my face against his and let him hear me purr.

Epilogue

That was a little over six months ago.

I'm not sure everyone completely believed our story of Fin's dramatic rescue of me from a crumbling rocky cliff, but we were welcomed back with more relief than anger. There were token punishments, but no imprisonment; Fin was moved to a different foster family, on a fish farm a couple of miles from Mealdarroch, and he now has much more freedom to roam the countryside.

Fin and I are panthers together about once a week, but we see each other much more often than that – in school, of course, and sometimes after and at weekends. He helps me with my homework, but he doesn't have to help me quite as much now. The teachers at Mealdarroch Academy are much better than the ones at my old school, the classes are smaller, and somehow, even with the accents, I am starting to catch on to things that never used to make sense. Even maths.

At Christmas I went back to Birmingham, to see my parents. I'd already made up my mind that I wanted to stay in Scotland. The suburban and city streets felt really strange, and a little frightening to me, and I couldn't imagine living there again. My

Mum was both pleased and sorry; she cried a lot, but kept saying she always knew I'd do well in the right school. She won't be in New York much longer, but she's not moving back to Birmingham, either. There's a possibility of a job in London. She and my Dad have decided to split up. The house is up for sale. I didn't see that much of my Dad at Christmas; he kept disappearing somewhere. Although he hasn't admitted it yet, I think he's got a girlfriend.

It's painful seeing my parents moving away into their different, separate lives, but I have a different life, too; one they don't know anything about.

Claire and I get along much better now, mostly, I think, because I am more interested in her, knowing her secret, and so I pay more attention, and try harder.

I still haven't told her about the animal spirit. I have been waiting for the right moment, and also afraid that the right moment will never come, and that whenever I do finally tell her, when she knows the truth at last, that she'll react badly. She may be too frightened to accept it, especially as it will mean understanding that she murdered a man when she shot that panther. But once she accepts the animal spirit, maybe she'll come to a deeper understanding. It's neither a crime nor a sin for an animal to kill, and Claire was acting in self-defence. Fin doesn't blame her; he says the old man practically forced her to shoot him. He had killed Lizzie, after all, and for all she knew he might have meant to kill her next.

I have to tell her, whatever the risk, because it would be awful never to know who you really are – and who else will tell her, if not me?

She may reject me, along with the news I bring. She could send me back to either my Mum or Dad, back to the cage of a city.

It makes me go cold, just to think of it, of losing everything, but I will do it. That is why I have written this book. Claire thinks I've been working on a project for school, night after night here at the computer my Dad bought me for Christmas. But it's not for school, it's for her, and for me. She might choose not to believe, she might want to think this is just a story. But it's my own story; the truth about both of us. Only the names have been changed; all of the facts are true.